THE INN OF DESTINY

INDIGO RIVER
PUBLISHING

THE INN OF DESTINY

A NOVEL

GENE P. ABEL

Indigo River Publishing

Indigo River Publishing
3 West Garden Street, Ste. 718
Pensacola, FL 32502
www.indigoriverpublishing.com

The Inn of Destiny | Gene P. Abel, author

ISBN: 978-1-950906-84-0 | LCCN: 2020918049
Edited by Tim Neller
Cover and interior design by Robin Vuchnich

Special discounts are available on quantity purchases by corporations, associations, and others. For details, contact the publisher at the address above.

Orders by US trade bookstores and wholesalers: Please contact the publisher at the address above.

With Indigo River Publishing, you can always expect great books, strong voices, and meaningful messages. Most importantly, you'll always find . . . words worth reading.

My sincere thanks to my beautiful wife, Susan Anne
for her help with my book.

1

The Inn

Jackie French was a young wife with natural red hair and beautiful blue eyes who lived with her husband, Jerry, in the affluent town of Princeton, New Jersey. Jackie and Jerry had two children: Lisa, who had just turned six, and David, who was eight. Jerry was an aspiring young financial executive working on Wall Street desperately trying to move higher into a six-figure income. The couple strove to live the good life, which they had done with astounding success. Like most couples, the challenge was to keep their relationship alive and fresh despite the pressure caused by modern life.

One fall morning Jackie said to Jerry, "We should do something different. We need to begin looking for an interesting weekend getaway for the two of us."

Jerry was engrossed in the morning paper and grunted some sort of affirmative signal, as he usually did at this time of day.

"Why aren't you more enthusiastic? Why must I always be the one to look for fun things to do?"

If the truth were known, Jackie really liked the role of arranger and enjoyed sitting down at the family computer to search the internet for some new adventure.

Lisa looked up and asked, "What will I do if you and Daddy go away for the weekend?"

David piped up, "We can go to Grammy and Pop Pop's."

Jackie was relieved at David's suggestion since she had talked with her mother about the children staying with them if they could get away for a weekend.

Midmorning, Jackie sat down at the computer and began looking at nearby areas for adventure. She came across the web page for the Inn of Destiny in the Pocono Mountains in nearby Pennsylvania. The web page was cleverly designed and portrayed the inn as a place where couples could have a unique and relaxing time away from their Monday-through-Friday routine.

Jackie picked up the phone and called the 800 number listed on the web page. She found that the only time that was available was the second weekend in February. Jackie asked the woman on the phone, "Can you hold that weekend for me until I talk it over with my husband?"

"I'm sorry. We had a very busy season, and I can't hold a room for you," the woman replied. "If you want to ensure accommodations, you'll have to let me know."

Without a second thought, Jackie said, "We'll take it. Do you need my credit card number?"

"Yes, please give me your number, and I will send you confirmation in the mail tomorrow."

After Jerry came home that evening, Jackie asked, "How would you like to go to the Poconos?"

Jerry nodded and said, "It's been a long time since I can remember going there. My father took me hunting in the mountains as a teenager."

"Well, take a look at what I found on the internet this morning, dear," responded Jackie. "I think this place is just what we're looking for."

Jerry began looking over the brightly colored pages Jackie had printed that morning before calling the inn. He laid them aside and said, "Why don't you give them a call sometime."

Jackie gave him that look he had seen so many times before that indicated she was up to something. "I called this morning, and they had only one weekend available this winter."

"I guess it must be a popular place. Oh well, if we can't go there this year, we can try again next year," Jerry said.

"We won't have to wait. I made a reservation for the second weekend in February."

Jerry seemed a little annoyed as he blurted out, "How do you know I don't have a conflict that weekend?"

"I looked at your calendar while I was on the phone with the lady at the inn," answered Jackie.

Jerry knew they needed this time alone together and decided to end his protest. He returned to reading his paper to catch up on the day's events.

The next morning, Jackie saw her neighbor and best friend Mary retrieving the morning paper from the lawn, where the delivery person had tossed it just minutes before. "Mary, what time will you be over for coffee?"

"I'll be right over," Mary answered.

It was their custom to have coffee together most mornings, and it wasn't long before Mary bounded into the kitchen through the back door. After some meaningless chatter about shopping and other trivial errands, their discussion turned to their lives in affluent Princeton. Mary's husband, John, was a contractor trying to build his net worth from the demand for new homes in nearby Bucks County, Pennsylvania. John was constantly looking for small- to midsize parcels of land that he could purchase and develop in order to move him closer and closer to the financial independence he sought.

Their conversation quickly turned to one of their favorite topics, which was how their husbands' quests for financial independence were affecting their love lives. Jackie and Mary were both in their early thirties and approaching the time when most women experience their greatest need for sexual fulfillment.

"Does Jerry have the same drive as when you met him?" Mary asked.

"No," answered Jackie. "He generally comes home from Wall Street, opens his briefcase, and works until midnight. During the week, he has very little desire for much physical activity and is focused on his busy schedule at the office. On the weekend, his interest shifts to either the kids, his golf game, or sports on TV. How is John in the romance department?"

Mary responded, "I often kid John that I feel like we're living in New England during the late 1700s and he's trying to become the perfect minuteman. He does seem to have an ample sex drive, but he seldom tries to get my temperature past lukewarm."

Jackie walked over to the desk in the kitchen and took out the material about the inn she'd printed from the internet. "Look at this, Mary. I took the bull by the horns to see if I can put a little zip into our sex life, even if it only lasts the weekend."

Mary read the material from the inn's web page and agreed that it was worth a shot. "Did you call them?" she asked.

"Not only did I call," answered Jackie, "but I reserved a weekend in February."

"What did Jerry say?"

"At first he seemed a little put out that I made the reservations without consulting him, but he seems to be looking forward to it now."

The early fall gave way to Thanksgiving and then to the Christmas season. It wasn't long before Jackie and Jerry would leave for their weekend in the Poconos. The second Friday in February finally arrived, and Jerry got ready to leave for the train. He reminded Jackie, "I'll be home early so that we can get on the road by three thirty."

"Fine," responded Jackie. "I'll take the kids to Mom when they get home from school."

Jackie then turned to getting Lisa and David ready for the school bus and cleaning up after breakfast. The day seemed to drag, as both Jackie and Jerry were looking forward to their weekend at the inn. Jerry had a meeting at lunch, which helped his day move along, and Jackie went with Mary to the department store. Jackie got home about two o'clock and finished packing for their trip. The kids arrived home a little after three, and she drove them to her mother's. Jackie wanted to be back by the time Jerry got home from the train station.

Jerry arrived from New York just before Jackie returned. They loaded the car and headed to Pennsylvania. Jerry decided to take the turnpike so they would arrive in the Poconos before dark. The clean snow on the mountains made their view look just like the travel brochures. As they passed mile after mile of split-rail fences, they couldn't help but admire the cows wandering in the fields. The gentle animals grazed on the grass hour after hour, just as if that was all the Creator ever intended for them to do. Some stroked their long tongues over the salt licks scattered in the fields. Jackie observed the breath of the cattle in the winter air and realized how cold it was in the mountains. As they passed farm after farm Jackie said, "How different the lifestyle is up here. I wonder if any of these people ever spend a weekend in New York."

Jackie noticed signs that depicted the type of corn that had been planted in the fields the past summer. She said, "Look at the ad for the candy factory. Let's see if we can find it tomorrow." As they drove higher into the mountains, they saw everything from tree farms to antique stores advertised on billboards. Every so often, they saw abandoned cars and trucks stacked in the fields. Next to these rusting carcasses of the twentieth century were bales of straw waiting to be picked up by farm trucks. It was about five o'clock when Jackie spotted a sign for the Inn of Destiny. "Oh, look, we're almost there."

As they passed through one more small town, they could see that time had not forgotten the area. The old rural town had been completed with its own strip mall. Jerry recalled the variety of wildlife that called these Pennsylvania state forests home. The deer population was extensive, and there were some bear and a few elk. The more patient visitor might even catch a glimpse of a small fox or a gray wolf.

As they climbed higher into the mountains, the number of farms lessened and the terrain became more rugged. They had rounded a bend in the road, when Jerry caught sight of a large log cabin in the distance. "Look, Jackie. I think that's the inn. It looks like the picture on the brochure you printed out."

A short way down the road was a sign announcing they had arrived. The log cabin was about two and a half stories high and stretched for hundreds of feet. The inn was constructed of the local timber that covered the mountains in this part of Pennsylvania. It was evident the inn had occupied this spot for decades.

Jerry saw the parking lot to the side and pulled in. "It doesn't look like there are many spaces available," he commented. There were a few spaces at the far end of the lot, so Jerry decided to drop their luggage off at the entrance and then find a parking space. The parking area was covered with snow and outlined with long pine logs. There was a break in the log barrier at the path that led to the main entrance.

As Jerry took Jackie's hand and led the way up the stairs to the front porch, Jackie remarked, "Look at how smooth the railing is. I wonder how many couples it took to wear it so smooth."

"More than you could count," was Jerry's response. "Look at this place. This door must be eight feet high and is made of two-inch-thick planks. The door latch looks like the ones we saw on the log cabins in Valley Forge Park."

The door latch was made of wood and leather and would indeed have been at home on the front door of Daniel Boone's homestead. Jerry lifted the latch and opened the massive door for Jackie.

The first thing she noticed was the fireplace with a roaring blaze that was framed by a mantel that contained beer steins from various places in the world. Above the log mantel was a large eight-point buck's head. The fireplace itself was made of fieldstone and was large enough to burn four-foot logs. Jackie moved closer to the blanket of heat that radiated from the fire. "This feels great. A warm fire always puts me in a romantic mood."

"Keep that mood alive for later. I'll see what I can do with it," Jerry responded. He was fully aware that Jackie had a strong romantic side that fed into her strong sex drive. It seemed that, as she crossed the thirty-year mark, her sexual desire had increased.

The couple turned from the welcoming fire to the large open area that housed the registration desk and lobby. The desk was typical and made from pine planks. It had a brass footrail along the front. There was a spittoon to one side, and at either end of the counter were cast-iron brackets used to scrape the mud from visitors' boots. When Jerry noticed that the counter was made using wooden pegs rather than nails, he commented, "I'll bet this place doesn't have a single nail in it." He was probably correct.

Everywhere one looked, the building seemed to be made using hand-fashioned joints and pegs. The floor appeared to be made of logs cut in half and secured with large wooden pegs. Remembering the crane used to lift the heavy roof of their house into place when it was built, Jackie looked at Jerry and asked, "How do you think they were able to hold the huge logs in place when they built the inn?"

Jerry walked to the registration counter. The clerk smiled warmly and said, "Welcome to the inn. We hope you will have a memorable weekend with us." He asked them to sign the registration book, which was held together by leather thongs. The pen was an old quill type complete with a brass ink well.

"Do you want me to use this pen?" asked Jerry.

"Yes, please," responded the clerk.

Behind the counter was a back bar that contained a fax machine, and the clerk entered their registration into a computer. A series of wooden boxes on the wall behind the counter held the hand-cut room keys.

"This place seems to be a blend of the past and the present," Jackie remarked.

She was right: the inn did combine both. Little did they realize some special guests would experience yet another dimension at the

Inn of Destiny. What was about to unfold would forever change the destinies of Jackie and Jerry French and their close friends. It would also begin a path for Jackie to stimulate her sensual side and desire for a more active sex life.

After Jerry completed registering, the printer prepared a listing that contained their names, date, and room assignment. It also listed some upcoming events for the evening and next day. This was another example of current technology in a vintage setting that their ancestors would not have recognized. The clerk reached into the fourth pigeonhole and took out the key to room D. As he handed it to Jerry, the expression on his face seemed to suggest this was more than simply giving them access to their room. Jackie noticed the clerk's expression but didn't comment. The clerk explained, "Take the right hall to the second door on the left. That will be room D."

As the couple made their way down the hall, they saw that there were twenty-six guest rooms. Each was identified by a letter from *A* to *Z*. When they found the door with a plaque that had the letter *D* carved on it, Jerry inserted the old key into the lock, opened the door, and was surprised when Jackie passed by him and bounded into the room.

The rustic room was lit by a single chandelier hanging from the ceiling. The walls were made of logs, and there was a fire burning in the fireplace. The rooms also had heaters, but the warm glow produced by the fire seemed so much more inviting. "They seem to be creating the perfect atmosphere for their guests," Jackie noted. "The web page was right. I think we're going to have a memorable weekend."

There was a four-poster bed made of—what else? —pine. It had a soft mattress with a large quilt at the foot of the bed. The curtains were made of heavy fabric to help keep out the frigid winds that blasted the inn during the long winter nights.

Jerry quickly changed his clothing and said, "I'll check out the bar while you change. Meet me there and we'll have a drink before dinner."

"Fine," replied Jackie. "I'll be down in about an hour. I want to relax in the whirlpool tub for a while before getting dressed."

Jerry proceeded to the bar, and Jackie got undressed as the tub filled with warm water.

As usual, Jackie's hour contained more than sixty minutes, but the time passed quickly, and Jerry greeted her as she walked into the bar. She wore a western-style shirt with a short denim skirt and completed her outfit with western boots. Jackie sat down at the bar and ordered a martini. Jerry asked for another bourbon.

When they finished their drinks, Jackie said, "I'm hungry. I never took time for lunch. There was just too much to get ready for our trip." They left the bar and entered the dining room, where they were seated near the large fireplace. It was made of the same fieldstone used in the other fireplaces. This one was used for cooking and had two large cast-iron pots hanging over the fire. The enticing aroma coming from these pots was the homemade soups that were part of the evening fare. Jackie turned to Jerry and commented, "This place keeps getting better and better. Do you think Mary and John would like to join us up here sometime? Maybe we could come together next winter."

After having a delicious meal, they decided to return to the bar, where a small combo was playing dance music. It was about nine thirty. Jackie remarked, "This small group does produce a great sound." They danced for two hours and had several drinks. Jackie made sure Jerry didn't overdo it. She had very definite plans for the remainder of the evening. While they were dancing, Jackie made sure Jerry was aware that she was not wearing a bra. In fact, she hadn't unpacked any of her underwear.

Just before the combo began to play their last song of the evening, Jackie walked over to the bar and sat on one of the stools. She discreetly parted her legs and, with her short skirt, gave Jerry a quick view of things to come. She was careful not to give every man in the room this same treat, but given her growing passion, she would not have minded if a select few men had caught her show.

At that point, Jerry was embarrassed to stand up. Jackie took one look at him and said, "I guess you liked my warm-up routine. I think we should go to our room." As they walked down the hall to their room, Jackie's anticipation of the romantic evening she had planned made her think of her first experiences with sex, the year she spent in Paris, and when she met Jerry.

2

Jackie's Passion Released

FROM THE TIME JACKIE had stopped playing with dolls, her thoughts turned to her developing female body. Her breasts began to develop in the sixth grade, and she would stand in front of her mirror and examine herself. As she progressed from a training bra to an A cup, her breasts had a sexy uplift as if they were reaching for the sky. From the time she was aware of her development, Jackie wanted the boys to notice her. Unlike some girls, Jackie wanted the boys to look at her bust and was disappointed if they only made eye contact with her.

By the ninth grade, Jackie had developed into a B cup and was able to attract the attention of the boys. Jackie was never crude but developed a seductive quality that only improved with age. She drove the boys crazy, for she appeared to be unreachable even though her body said *come get me*. This fed Jackie's growing sexuality and desire to be sought after. Jackie's best friend, Darlene, was a natural blonde and was only slightly behind Jackie in her physical development. Starting with Jackie's junior year, she and Darlene sought subtle ways to tease the boys. Neither girl was sexually active, but they were both moving closer to their first sexual experience.

On one occasion, Jackie decided to cut the tip of her bra so it would appear that she wasn't wearing a bra. The boys knew she was wearing a bra by the straps, but from the front it looked like she wasn't. Seeing what Jackie had done, Darlene didn't want to be outshined and removed the entire cup of her bra. This left only the supports that surrounded her breasts and the straps. The day she wore this bra to school she drove the boys wild. Jackie saw what Darlene had done and asked her what she planned to do next. Darlene told her to wait and see. It was this type of give-and-take that made them such good friends, and they didn't consider each other competition. After all, there were many studs at their high school, and, up to this point, Jackie and Darlene had not fixated on the same boy.

Both Jackie and Darlene were almost as intrigued with the male body as they were with their own. The sexual tension was building to a point where they began talking about how they would be initiated into sexual activity. Jackie discovered a box of the most explicit romance novels in her attic. She brought them into her room and hid them in her closet. She began reading and would lend them to Darlene as she finished each book. The girls would then discuss the various sexual encounters that were described in these novels. By the time they had read the twenty or so novels, they were well on their way to having read and discussed almost every type of erotic pleasure. All this added to the sexual frustration of both girls.

Jackie began to fondle her breasts and private female areas in an effort to relieve some of her tension. It wasn't long before Jackie was able to satisfy herself. She could not believe the pleasure that gave her. The next day, she asked Darlene if she'd had a similar experience. Darlene informed her that she'd had her first experience about the time she finished reading the first novel Jackie had given her. By the middle of her junior year, Jackie had reached a C cup and her satisfaction from self-gratification was no longer enough. During the Christmas recess, Jackie and Darlene decided to have a sleepover at Darlene's house. They began talking about how they would arrange losing their virginity. Darlene had been snooping in her older brother's room and come across a XXX video. About 10:00 p.m., Darlene decided to show the tape to Jackie.

"Where did you get this?" Jackie asked.

"Oh, from my brother's room," Darlene answered. She put the tape in her VCR and turned the sound very low so her parents wouldn't hear the distinctive moans that were part of the activities. They were glued to the screen as they saw many of the things they had read about in the romance novels. It wasn't long before Darlene began imitating what the actors were doing on the TV. Darlene looked over to see what Jackie was doing and reached over and began touching her. At first, Jackie seemed startled but allowed Darlene to have her way. It wasn't long before Darlene removed Jackie's top to give her the same treatment. Jackie and Darlene continued watching the erotic scenes and imitating everything they saw as it was being done on-screen. Although both girls had a stimulating time, they decided they weren't comfortable with having sex with another female. Because of this lesbian encounter, they began to plan their first sexual encounters with males.

The girls were cheerleaders and decided to double date. They arranged to have the boys meet them after a basketball game so they would be in their cheerleader outfits. They knew it was almost every boy's fantasy to have sex with a cheerleader. After the game, Jackie, Stan, Darlene, and Joe arranged to meet and go for a snack at the local diner. After they finished eating, Jackie and Darlene went in the restroom and removed their panties. They stuffed their pants in their purses, and wearing nothing under their short skirts, they rejoined their dates.

They drove to one of the more secluded parking spots. Joe was the first to learn that Darlene had removed her underpants when he accidentally caught the edge of Darlene's dress in his watchband and pulled her skirt up. He wanted to tell Stan but decided that wasn't a good idea. He wasn't sure if Jackie had done the same thing, or if this was just something that Darlene had done. Joe began to French kiss Darlene, which really turned her on. She loved the feel of his tongue on her tongue, and the final barrier of her resistance quickly melted away.

She signaled her consent by slowly parting her legs and removing her blouse. After Darlene unhooked her bra, the short cheerleading skirt was the only clothing on her striking body. Darlene opened Joe's belt, slid down his zipper, and removed his jeans. She pulled down his jockey shorts, and they became lost in the pleasure of each other.

Jackie was more forceful in the front seat and placed Stan's hand under her skirt to reveal her naked body. Stan was a bit surprised. In the past, Jackie had only allowed him to engage in some light petting. She had never indicated that she was ready to initiate total sexual activity. Stan found Jackie eager to begin moving through the bases. For the first few minutes, he was careful not to actually make contact with her most private parts, but this only drove Jackie through the roof. She decided it was time for Stan to practice some of the moves shown in the XXX videos and began doing everything she could to please Stan. Before long, she realized that Stan was about to explode. Her first instinct was to stop, but she knew that wasn't what Stan wanted, so she continued until Stan indicated she should stop. Jackie was apprehensive when she saw Stan during round one. She wondered how that thing was going into her. Her concern was well founded. As with most girls, Jackie found her first encounter with intercourse somewhat painful and accompanied by some bleeding.

However, Stan recovered quickly, and it was no time before he was ready for round two. He slowly began to engage in foreplay to try to move Jackie into a state of excitement. He used the missionary position with Jackie and continued until he climaxed. They remained entangled with each other for some time after they completed their lovemaking.

Joe managed to arouse Darlene through manual stimulation while passionately kissing her. She returned the favor by mounting him and had the same unpleasant first experience with intercourse as Jackie. Stan and Joe assured the girls that their next experience with intercourse would produce the pleasure that was depicted in the XXX videos they watched. Because they didn't want to risk becoming pregnant, both girls had started taking a birth control pill. They preferred the pill and didn't want their first sexual experiences complicated by other forms of birth control. After the two couples finished, they got dressed and went for ice cream. When they finished eating, the guys dropped the girls off at Darlene's house.

Jackie had arranged to sleep over at Darlene's. The girls were greeted by Darlene's parents and proceeded up to the bedroom. The two girls stayed up most of the night comparing notes. Their planning had certainly resulted in their first sexual experiences with a boy. Jackie had other sexual encounters with Stan during the balance of her junior year. All but one of those times, Stan was successful in satisfying Jackie. It was clear: he had a fair amount of prior experience and always tried to please the girl during sex. Jackie soon learned that she experienced the strongest satisfaction when brought on by manual stimulation. She allowed Stan to choose the technique he wanted, but she did let him know what pleased her the most. Near the end of her junior year, Jackie was still experimenting with what pleased her and decided to see if Stan would agree to a threesome with a second guy. At first, Stan was not too keen on a threesome with two guys, but eventually he agreed so long as the other guy wasn't one of his close friends. They talked about several possible candidates and finally settled on Bill. He was about the same build as Stan but blond. Stan didn't know Bill very well and found it a bit hard to breach this subject with him. When he finally did have the opportunity to talk with him, Bill eagerly agreed when he found out Jackie was involved.

They set the date up for the next Saturday night and decided to go to the local drive-in. They found a space in the last row, which afforded them more privacy. Stan went for some sodas, and Jackie and Bill began talking. They decided to get into the back seat and were just starting to kiss when Stan returned with the sodas. He too got in the rear seat and handed Jackie and Bill their drinks. Jackie decided to get things rolling by unzipping Bill's fly and then Stan's. Jackie discovered Bill was very well endowed. Jackie didn't want to make Stan feel inadequate and made sure to give the boys equal attention. The three made love for several hours, and by the time they finished, the guys knew every part of Jackie's outstanding body. For Jackie's part, she got a real high from being able to satisfy both of them. Jackie felt a bit embarrassed when the two guys fondled her as they watched the movie. Before long, Jackie asked if they would take her home, and all got dressed and left the movie.

Jackie wanted to see Bill again but on a one-to-one basis. They arranged to spend the night at his house on a weekend while his mother and father were out of town. Bill called for a pizza, and in about twenty minutes it arrived. They ate the pizza, and then Jackie decided to do a striptease for Bill. She got down to a small red thong, went over to him sitting on the floor, and told him to remove the thong. Bill obliged her. He then went over to the TV and began to play an XXX video he had rented for the night's encounter.

It didn't take long before Bill, too, was naked, and they began exploring every part of each other. Jackie decided to get on top of Bill. He knew, in that position, Jackie was controlling the action, and he could only last as long as she chose. *No matter*, he thought. *I'm good for three times, so let her have her way.* Jackie didn't experience a climax in that position, but she knew that she was indeed in control, which made her feel good.

They resumed looking at the video, and in a short time, Bill began caressing Jackie's breasts. It didn't take long for Bill to expand his attention to her most sensitive areas. This brought Jackie the ultimate moment of pleasure, after which Bill decided to achieve his objective.

The video was showing a threesome similar to the one they'd had with Stan. In about fifteen minutes, Bill began to show signs of new life and they again made love. At this point, Bill was getting tired and they decided to end their romantic evening with some ice cream. As it turned out, that was the last time Jackie dated Bill. She had satisfied her fantasy with this big stud and had a chance to experience sex in new and interesting ways. Jackie continued to date Stan throughout the summer.

Stan's father had a 1976 Cadillac convertible that Jackie loved. On a few occasions, Stan was able to borrow his father's car for a date with Jackie. She felt special in that car. While they were cruising with the top down, Jackie suggested that they have another threesome. Stan said he was up for that, but this time he wanted it to be two girls. Jackie decided that was OK, so Stan set it up for a weekend when his parents were out of town. After Jackie agreed to this threesome with another girl, she began to have second thoughts. She didn't like the idea of competing for Stan's attention, and she wasn't sure how she felt about having another female touch her. True, she'd had one lesbian affair with her girlfriend, but that was something that had just happened. Nevertheless, Jackie decided to go through with it, and the Friday night arrived.

Jackie prepared by taking a long bath in scented bath salts. She wanted to be at her best for Stan and to make sure she was the better of the two girls in this threesome. Jackie didn't want to know who the second girl was until they picked her up. Jackie insisted Stan get her first and then stop for the other girl. As it turned out, Stan had arranged to have an attractive girl by the name of Rachael as the second girl. She was an athletic girl with true blonde hair. Stan would be in seventh heaven—a redhead and a blonde at the same time!

Stan picked Jackie up about eight, and then they went to pick up Rachael. She was waiting in front of her house and got in the front seat next to Jackie. She, too, was wearing an enticing scent, although it was different from the one Jackie was wearing. *Good thing*, Jackie thought. *Stan will be able to tell us apart in the dark.* They arrived at Stan's house, and he opened the garage door with the remote. They got out and went into the house through the garage. Jackie had decided to wear underwear, and had on a short skirt, a loose-fitting top, and sandals without stockings. Rachael was dressed in a see-through two-piece chiffon dress that enabled one to see her thong and delicate lace bra. She, too, wore sandals without stockings. Although Jackie didn't know Rachael, she had heard that she did have a bit of a reputation. From the way she was dressed, Jackie thought it must be true.

In reality, Jackie was a bit more aggressive than Rachael was. The difference was that Jackie was more careful to only display her feelings in private. This was the first time Rachael had been involved in a three-way sexual encounter. However, Rachael was a bit AC/DC and had no problems with making love to another female. Stan told the girls to get comfortable in the family room while he got some refreshments. They sat on the sofa while Stan got some soda and chips. Stan had gotten an XXX-rated video that had three-way sex involving two other girls. He thought this would break the ice and show how the characters on the screen got it on. Before they started to play the video, Jackie suggested they play ten hands of strip poker to get started. She hoped that Rachael would lose so she could get a better look at her competition.

Stan and Rachael thought that was a great idea and Stan got a deck of cards. The first hand didn't go as Jackie expected. Rachael won, and she and Stan each had to remove one item of clothing. Stan took off his shirt and Jackie removed one of her sandals. The second hand went to Stan, and Jackie lost her second sandal while, much to her surprise, Rachael chose to remove her top to reveal her very ample breasts. The third hand also went to Stan, and this time Jackie removed her blouse, while Rachael decided on a sandal. By the tenth hand, Rachael was only wearing a thong and Jackie decided to give up everything except her bra.

She knew her most outstanding body part was her breasts, and she wanted to prolong the suspense. The real question was, Prolonging the suspense for whom? Since Stan was well aware of how beautiful her breasts were, it seemed this was more for Rachael's benefit. Stan had fared well in the strip poker and only lost his shirt, socks, and sneakers. Stan started the video and began the visual aid. The three spent about twenty minutes only looking at the video and went through one complete threesome. As the second session began, Stan went to the kitchen to get some props. He returned with a squeeze bottle of chocolate sauce and a can of whipped cream. Although this was not used in the video, Stan thought this was a great way to get started.

Rachael removed Jackie's bra and began applying the chocolate sauce to her. She then began removing it with her tongue. Stan decided it was time for him to participate in the activities. At this point, Jackie put the chocolate all over Stan and added a dab of whipped cream. She began licking the sauce from Stan, and it wasn't long before Jackie tasted something other than chocolate sauce. Stan responded by applying the chocolate to Jackie and showing her the pleasure of a total cleanup.

Jackie commented, "Too bad you don't have a cherry for your treat."

Rachael decided to help Stan remove the sundae from Jackie, and the duel attention soon culminated in Jackie's moment of pleasure. They returned to watching the video for a while to give Stan a chance to recover. After about a half hour, Rachael began teasing Stan and was able to bring him back into action. Stan and Jackie decided it was time for Rachael to be the sundae and experience the intense pleasure they had enjoyed. Just as she completed her ecstasy, she decided to have sex with Stan to finish off her pleasure.

Rachael began to caress Jackie. Stan chose to observe the interaction between the two girls and didn't take part. Jackie began to feel a bit uncomfortable with Rachael touching her and asked her to stop. Stan finally suggested they all take a shower to clean off the chocolate sauce. The master bath had a two-person shower with dual showerheads. They decided to try it for three. Stan was eager to make sure all the chocolate and whipped cream was washed from every part of the girls. They were just as eager to make sure Stan was squeaky clean from top to bottom. They completed their shower and got dressed. Rachael wanted to walk the two blocks to her house, and Stan drove Jackie home.

After this encounter, Jackie knew she didn't want another lesbian experience. Soon after that evening, Jackie and Stan ended their relationship, and Jackie set her sights on a placekicker named Rick. It didn't take Jackie long to attract Rick's attention, and she began seeing him at the start of her senior year.

3

Jackie in Paris

JACKIE WAS A GIRL who knew what she wanted and, for the most part, how to get it. She wasn't shy when it came to meeting new people or experiencing new things, or when it came to her physical relationships. She attended Smith College, a small, private liberal-arts school in Northampton, Massachusetts, and one of the few remaining schools whose principal objective was undergraduate education for women. The 125-acre campus housed twenty-five hundred undergraduate females as well as several hundred graduate coeds. Jackie's parents were pleased she decided to attend Smith because they thought that the mostly female population would allow Jackie to concentrate on her education.

Although this was the case, the male students attending the prestigious universities in New England were well aware of Smith and the twenty-five hundred girls on campus, mostly from well-to-do families. The program at Smith included an option to study abroad during junior year. In fact, almost one quarter of the junior class participated in this program. Jackie had decided to study in Paris, and that was one of the reasons she chose Smith. Jackie loved art, which was the primary reason she selected Paris for her overseas study. Little did she know her year abroad would enhance her academic studies and give her a better sense of what she wanted from life. Even though the Smith students were supervised while abroad, they had many opportunities to experience life in their host countries.

One such case for Jackie was her relationship that developed with François. He was a twenty-nine-year-old artist whose outstanding talent hadn't been discovered yet. Jackie was seated alone at a small outdoor cafe just around the corner from where she lived. She was having a drink of bottled water when she first saw François. He had his ever-present drawing pad under his arm as he strolled down the sidewalk across from the café. They seemed to notice each other about the same time, and there was an instant connection. Jackie noticed his great butt and the friendly expression on his face. As for François, Jackie's red hair and striking body were all he needed to spring into action.

He crossed the small street and approached her table. "Parlez-vous français?" he asked.

Although Jackie had taken French as part of her studies at Smith, she shook her head no.

François spoke almost perfect English but chose to use a broken style of English at first. "American, yes?"

Jackie nodded.

"Join you?"

This time Jackie responded, "If you must."

"Are you here on holiday?" he asked.

"No. I'm studying for a year in Paris. My college has a program that includes study abroad during the third year of school." Jackie took one look at his pad and the leather pouch that held his drawing equipment and said, "I guess you must be the local artist."

"Well, I don't know about the local part, but yes, I am an artist," François responded.

He was apparently familiar with the café, as he called the waiter by name. He ordered two glasses of wine and some cheese with a loaf of French bread. Jackie understood what he had ordered and was surprised by his action. However, she hadn't eaten lunch and wanted to learn more about this attractive Frenchman.

The waiter returned in a few minutes with a tray containing the wine, cheese, and warm bread.

"What is this?" Jackie asked.

"I thought you might like some refreshment. You are so skinny. You must not eat very much."

Almost automatically, Jackie said, "I'm too fat."

Nothing was further from the truth, as François knew from his first glance at her. If anything, Jackie could have used a few pounds. They began to eat the bread and cheese as they questioned each other about their lives. Jackie became more interested as François described his life in Paris. Gradually it became evident that he did, in fact, have a firm command of English. On the other hand, Jackie did not tip her hand as to her understanding of French.

"Where are you staying while in Paris?" he asked.

"I share an apartment around the corner at Twelve rue Royal. I live there with my roommate from Smith."

"Smith? Is that the name of your school?" François asked.

"Yes. It is in Massachusetts."

"That is in your New England, yes?"

"That's right. It's a girls' school. We have about twenty-five hundred students attending the undergraduate school."

"You mean there are no male students, just girls?"

"That's right. Except for a few graduate students, it is all girls."

"Sounds like heaven," was his response. "Why did you choose to have a roommate?" François inquired.

"Well, my parents didn't want me to live alone, so Barb is my roommate. She's a lot of fun, and we do everything together."

"Did you say 'everything'?"

"Well, not quite everything," Jackie answered.

As they finished their repast, it was clear there was an instant attraction between them. "Would you like to see my flat? You could see some of my drawings," François asked. Normally Jackie wouldn't have been so quick to say yes, but she liked François and was interested in seeing his drawings.

"Sure. Is it far from here?"

"It's two stops on the Métro. Have you used it?"

"Yes, Barb drags me all over Paris on it," Jackie replied.

François paid the waiter, and they walked to the Métro entrance. The two stops passed quickly, and they emerged from the subway into the muted light of an early spring afternoon. The weather was typical for that time of year, not great but OK. François led the way to his flat. He bounded up the stairs two at a time and opened the door for Jackie. The doorway led into a vestibule and to the stairs. His flat was on the third floor of this older row home that was of an earlier age. It was easy to see the quality of this home and the detail in the design. Each flat had fireplaces in the living room, den, and bedroom. The woodwork was superb, and the hardwood floors were beautiful. The ceilings were ornate, and the doors were solid wood.

"Do you live alone?" Jackie asked.

"Yes. I like to be able to come and go as I please. I often work at odd hours. Generally, I draw during the best light of day, but sometimes I add finishing touches at night by the fireplace light," François explained.

"I know what you mean; the one thing about having a roommate is that you must think of what they are doing before you plan something in your apartment."

François had his studio in a room off the living room. Jackie walked toward the partially open door to the studio and peered into the room. There was a skylight that poured light into the room, and Jackie could see scores of drawings along the walls. A sofa was in the center of the room with some assorted furniture surrounding it. An easel that held a partially completed drawing was in front of the sofa. It was immediately apparent: François sketched old buildings and nude girls. It appeared that most of the nudes had been drawn on the sofa in the room.

François saw Jackie looking into the room and said, "Please go in and look at my work."

"Are you sure?" Jackie asked.

"Go, go."

Jackie opened the door and walked into his studio. She was surprised by the quality of his work. He drew in a style called photo realism. His drawings looked like photographs, and his use of shading gave many of them a three-dimensional quality. He used charcoal and pencils. Only one of his sketches was done in color.

François asked, "Can I get you something?"

"Yes, a bottle of water would be fine."

He went to the kitchen and returned with two bottles of spring water.

"Your drawings are so real. I see you don't use much color."

"I use color only when I am happy with my work," he responded.

The number of nude women François had drawn surprised Jackie. He saw her blush as she examined his nudes. There were at least ten different girls in his drawings. One particular girl must have been special, for he had over a dozen sketches of her. Jackie would not have been surprised if these models had started to talk, they were so lifelike.

"How long have you been drawing?" Jackie asked.

"Ever since I can remember. My family always gave me drawing supplies for gifts. I would draw almost anything that caught my attention from the time I attended grammar school," François responded.

"Did you have any formal training?"

"Yes, several artists I met at the Louvre worked with me for the past two years."

Françoise saw that Jackie was embarrassed by some of his drawings, and he tried to make her feel more at ease. "The French do not have the same shyness about nudity as you Americans. Many French girls pose in the nude with no more reluctance than if I took your picture right now with your clothing on."

Jackie sat on a small stool and looked at a sketch detailing the front door of Notre Dame. François's drawing concentrated on the gargoyles that adorned the doorway. He explained, "When this church was built in the thirteenth century, there was still the vestige of pre-Christian superstition in France. The gargoyles were intended to protect the church from evil spirits."

Jackie got up and walked to the far wall where a stack of nudes had been placed. The drawings captured every detail and curve of the girls' bodies. The shading made them look even more real. It didn't matter whether you looked at the light in their eyes, the curve of their necks, the areolas surrounding their nipples, or their pubic areas; all were depicted with reverence and accuracy.

Jackie finished looking at the sketches and decided it was time to go back to her apartment. François took her back to 12 rue Royal and said goodbye at the front door of her building. Several weeks passed, and then Jackie found a note from François on her apartment door. The note had his telephone number on it and said, *Would you like to go cycling with me on Saturday? I will pick you up Saturday at ten unless I hear from you.* Jackie thought he was a bit overconfident, but decided to take him up on his offer.

At a little after ten Saturday morning, there was a knock at their apartment door. Jackie was still in the bathroom, so Barbara answered the door. François introduced himself, and Barb asked him to come in and wait for Jackie. Although Jackie was actually ready, she had decided to keep him waiting for a few minutes to give Barb a chance to look him over.

François asked Barbara, "How do you like Paris?"

"It's great. I plan to return some day after I've completed college."

François thought to himself that Barb was a very attractive blonde, but she was not in the same league as Jackie.

In about fifteen minutes, Jackie emerged from the bathroom and came over to François. He stood up and asked Jackie, "Are you ready to go?"

"Sure," she answered. "I'll see you tonight, Barb."

They went to the door and François turned to Barb and said, "Au revoir. It was nice meeting you." François had his car parked in front of Jackie's flat with two bicycles strapped to the top. They got into the car and took off for the country. François's driving was like all the other French that Jackie had encountered. They all seemed to drive like a bat out of hell.

Jackie asked, "Where are we going riding?"

"I thought we would get away from Paris and drive north to the countryside. The small French towns are so picturesque."

Jackie had not been outside of Paris, and she was glad he had chosen the country for their cycling. She expected that small towns would be very different from Paris, and the change was a welcome one for her.

It was about eleven thirty when François pulled the car into a rest area near the town of Clermont. He removed the bicycles from the roof of the car and strapped a lunch basket and his sketchpad on the back of his cycle. They started down the small country lane. As they rode down the two-lane path, François asked, "Do you ride in the States?"

"Sometimes. I usually go to the spa for my exercise," Jackie said.

François wanted to flatter her and said, "It shows. You have the most perfect figure that I have ever seen."

Jackie was a little embarrassed by his comment, but she quickly said, "I'll take that as a compliment, given all the beautiful girls you have seen."

They continued down the road for about an hour before they stopped in a meadow for lunch. François spread a blanket on the grass and laid out the lunch he'd prepared. There was an assortment of meats and cheese as well as the ever-present French bread. He had also brought some wine and bottled water. They spent half an hour eating their lunch and talking about their lives.

After lunch, François asked Jackie if he could sketch her lying on the blanket. Given the beautiful women he was accustomed to using for models, Jackie was flattered by his request. "Sure," she answered. "I would like to pose for you, as long as I can keep my clothing on."

"Please lie on your side. I will cover the basket with part of the blanket and make a rest for your head. I want you to be comfortable. It will take me about an hour to complete the essentials. I will fill in the details later at my studio."

Jackie got comfortable and François began to sketch her beautiful face.

About an hour had passed when François announced, "I have enough for now. We should start back."

It was four o'clock when they arrived at the car. François fastened the bicycles on the roof, and they began the drive back to Paris.

When they arrived at François's flat, it was getting dark.

"How about going to dinner with me," he asked.

"Barb is expecting me home early," replied Jackie.

But François persisted, saying, "Why don't you call her and tell her we are having dinner together."

"I need to freshen up after our ride."

"You can use the bath, and my sister has some clothing in the apartment that should fit you."

"Are you sure? Don't you think your sister would mind a stranger using her clothing?"

"Not at all," François insisted.

Jackie used the phone in François's studio so she would have a little privacy. "Barb, guess what? He asked me to dinner. What do you think I should do?"

"What will you wear?" Barb asked. "You must be a mess after the bike ride."

"He offered to let me use his bath and borrow some clothing of his sister's he has here."

Barb was a little surprised, but she said, "Whatever you think is best. You did say you liked him. This will give you a chance to get to know him better."

"I'll see you tonight," Jackie told Barb.

"Yes, if the sun doesn't come up too early!"

"You're bad. I will not spend the night, at least not on the first date. See you." They said goodbye and hung up.

As Jackie came out of the studio, François greeted her with two of his sister's dresses. "Take your pick. You will look sensational in either one. In fact, you would look great in anything."

Jackie chose a beige dress with a scooped neck and a skirt that came just above the knee. He showed her the tub and gave her some fresh towels. The first thing Jackie noticed was the bidet. She did not comment as François walked to the tub and began drawing her bath water. She hung the dress on a hook fastened to the wall and led François to the bathroom door. It was as if he was hoping for an invitation to help her take a bath. She was not about to make such an offer.

She added some bath salts and finished filling the tub. She wondered why he had all those great-smelling bath salts. Could it be that she was not the first female guest to use his tub? Jackie had soaked about half an hour when she again noticed the bidet. She recalled overhearing stories her grandfather had told about this appliance. During World War I, the American doughboys were surprised to see the French prostitutes wash themselves on the bidet after servicing them. Many of the American soldiers came from farms where they didn't even have inside plumbing much less a bidet. The sight of a naked woman mounted on this thing washing her private parts was unexpected to say the least. The rumor was that the bidet not only fulfilled a practical need but also gave the women pleasure as well.

Jackie decided that, although she was not in need of any further cleaning, she would give it a try to see if the rumor was true. She got out of the tub and walked over to the bidet. Jackie tried the spigots so she would know how it operated. She mounted it and turned on the water. To her delight, the feeling of the water gushing into her was titillating. She knew why this bathroom fixture was so popular in Europe. She wondered why this wasn't more popular with American women. François heard the sound of Jackie using the bidet, and he couldn't help but picture her sitting on it. This thought stayed with him for some time.

It took Jackie another half an hour to complete her bath. She decided not to wear her soiled underwear and put her panties and bra in her purse. Jackie often went without a bra, but she normally wore small bikini panties.

When she came out of the bathroom, François took one look at her and said, "You look fantastic. My sister, Babette, never filled out that dress the way you do!"

Jackie began to blush and said, "You better be careful. I will tell her what you said."

François took some clean clothing from his bedroom and went into the bathroom. Unlike Jackie, François took only twenty minutes to bathe and get dressed. While he was in the bathroom, Jackie read some of his magazines about French artists. When François came out of the bathroom and saw her reading the books, which were in French, he said, "I thought you did not understand French."

"Oh, well, I didn't want you to know everything about me at once."

By the time they arrived at the restaurant, it was about eight o'clock. That was a perfect time to begin dinner in Paris. Since François now knew that Jackie understood his language, she ordered her menu in French. Dinner lasted two hours, and when they finished François asked if she wanted to take a cab or walk in the cool spring air.

"Let's walk," Jackie suggested.

"That's fine," he agreed. François paid the waiter, and they were on their way. When they got to his flat, François said, "Would you like a night cap?" By this time, Jackie was relaxed with François. She decided to take him up on his offer.

They climbed the two flights of stairs, and François opened the door for Jackie.

She looked around and said, "Where is my portrait?"

François reached into the closet and pulled out his tablet that contained the sketch he had started that afternoon.

Jackie was surprised when she looked at it, and said, "You've only completed my face. When will you do the rest of me?"

"Well, how about now?"

"Only if you have some good wine," replied Jackie. "It always puts me in a relaxed mood."

"Please take a seat on the sofa," responded François. "I'll be right back with your wine."

François returned in a few minutes and said, "Lie on your side like you were this afternoon." He placed her portrait on the easel and began to sharpen his pencils. Jackie wondered if he would ask her to undress and contemplated what she would say if he did. She didn't have to wait very long.

François came from behind his easel and sat on the edge of the sofa next to her. "I would like to complete your portrait in the nude."

Jackie looked up into his face and asked, "Will you give me the drawing when it's complete?"

"If you like," he responded. François reached down and slowly began to undo the buttons that started at the collar and ended at the bottom of her skirt. It soon became evident Jackie was not wearing a bra. He already knew she didn't have one on by the way her breasts poked through her dress. However, he was surprised to find her naked stomach as he opened the buttons at her waist. By this time Jackie was blushing, and it seemed like a lifetime until François opened the last several buttons to reveal her dark red patch.

He removed her dress, which enabled him to see the true extent of her beautiful body. It was a sight to behold. He thought to himself, *I have never had a sexier model. She is exquisite.* He couldn't wait to capture her likeness on paper and began his labor of love.

Jackie's long red hair fell lightly over her shoulders as if to guide his eyes to her uplifted breasts. She was a C cup that seemed to poke upward toward the ceiling. Her waist was small but not so small that it looked out of proportion to her hips. She had a flat tummy and perfectly shaped legs that led to her delicate feet to round out this five-foot-six beauty from America.

"Lie more on your side. Rest your right arm on the seat of the sofa, and place your left arm on the top of the sofa back. Bend your left leg, and place your foot on the seat of the sofa, and extend your right leg." This pose placed Jackie in about the same position she was in when he started her sketch. It also enabled him to capture all of her outstanding body.

"Is this the way you draw all your nudes?"

François responded, "Each model is special. I try to capture that in all my drawings. No two women have the same body. That's what makes drawing nude women so fascinating."

It took him about an hour to complete the sketch of her body. When he finished, Jackie took the clothing she wore when they went cycling and got dressed.

"You are welcome to stay the night even if you insist on sleeping alone. You can use my bed, and I will sleep on the sofa," he said.

"No, thanks. I told Barb I would be home tonight."

They walked to his car and he drove Jackie home.

When they arrived at 12 rue Royal, she thanked him for a wonderful day and started to get out of the car.

"I will call you just as soon as I complete the details on your portrait," François said. Walking her to the door, he gave her a gentle kiss on the lips. "Au revoir."

"Au revoir," she responded. He got back in his car as she went in her door. She watched as he drove away and thought, I cannot remember a better day in Paris!

Several weeks passed, and Jackie began to wonder if François would ever call her. Had she become just another portrait in his collection? As lifelike as his drawings were, it was as if he had taken a nude photograph of her. That reminded her of the nude pictures she had allowed her high school boyfriend Rick to take of her. She often wondered if he still had those pictures, or if some other guy was looking at them.

Rick and Jackie were an item in high school, especially during their senior year. Rick was a placekicker on the football team. He was a bit headstrong, but Jackie was able to keep control of their relationship. That was surely the case when it came to sex. Most of the time, she would allow Rick to go only so far. Generally, when they were out parking, she would allow him to slip his hand under her bra or take it off, giving him complete access to her breasts. During the entire time they were going together, Jackie only allowed Rick to go all the way a few times. It was during one such occasion, in Rick's bedroom, that Jackie allowed him to take nude pictures of her using his father's Polaroid camera. Rick and Jackie had a lot of fun together, but their relationship ended when Rick was admitted to Penn State and she chose Smith. Jackie hadn't heard from Rick since the middle of their freshman year. At this point, the only thing that made her remember him were those nude pictures.

About a week later, the telephone rang. Barb answered, "Hello?"

"Bonjour. It's François. Is Jackie there?"

"No. She's out shopping for groceries."

"Will you ask her to call me when she gets home?"

"Sure thing. Goodbye."

Jackie returned carrying two bags of food. Barb greeted her at the door and said, "Who do you think called you?"

"François," answered Jackie. "What did he say?"

"He wants you to call him."

"He must have my picture finished." Because they were very close and told each other everything, Jackie had told Barb about the nude portrait. "I can't wait to see it," Jackie remarked.

She put the two bags on the table and took the phone over to the sofa to call François. The phone rang seven times, and Jackie had decided he was out. Just as she was about to hang up, François answered, "Bonjour?"

"Hi. It's Jackie. Barb said you called. How have you been?"

"Very busy. I secured a commission to draw some landmarks in Paris, which I just completed. How is school?"

"About like your art. I handed in two papers that I've been working on for over a month. Have you had a chance to finish my portrait?"

"Yes, I have," answered François. "How about coming over Saturday to get it?"

"OK. What time?"

"How does two o'clock sound?"

"Great. I'll see you then. Goodbye."

"Au revoir," he replied.

Jackie was on a high after her call.

"What did he say?" Barb asked.

"My portrait is finished. He wants me to come over on Saturday and pick it up. I don't know if I can wait!"

Both girls were so excited they decided to get dinner at the café where Jackie first met François.

On Saturday morning, Jackie had some last-minute work to finish for school and tried to complete it before she had to leave for François's. This proved to be an impossible task. All she could think about was her picture.

"Why does time seem to move so slowly when you want something?" Jackie asked.

"I know what you mean," Barb replied. "There are other times when time seems to fly."

Jackie chose to be a little dressier and wore a brown silk blouse and a knee-length tan skirt. She also wore a wide dark-brown belt that accented her figure. Jackie completed the outfit with leather sandals. About one thirty, she picked up her purse and said goodbye to Barb. It was raining lightly, and she decided to take a small umbrella along. As she stepped through the front door of her apartment, she opened the umbrella and began to walk toward the Métro.

It was just after two when she arrived at François's flat. He was looking for her out of his third-floor window. He wondered if she really knew the Métro stops as well as she said she did. Apparently, she had mastered the subway. He came down the stairs and greeted her at the front door. "You found it," he said.

"Didn't you think I would be able to find you?"

"Well, I was not sure," François admitted. He was glad to see her, and it seemed Jackie couldn't get up to the apartment fast enough. In fact, she was so excited she ran up the stairs with her umbrella still up. "Do you think it is raining in here?" François wanted to know.

Jackie waited in the living room while François got her portrait. He hadn't mounted it because he thought it would be easier for her to take rolled up. He handed her the picture, and she saw he had done it in color. She took one look at his work and said, "Oh my God! I have never seen anything so beautiful!" There was little doubt this would leave most people speechless. The drawing captured every detail of Jackie's outstanding body, including her red hair and deep blue eyes. François had captured the faint freckles that began on Jackie's face and continued down her chest, her breasts, and her stomach, to her shapely legs until they stopped short of her feet.

"What do you think?" François asked.

"I can't believe it. It looks like I'm looking at myself in the mirror. In fact, it's better than that," she remarked.

"I take it you approve?"

"Yes!" she exclaimed. At that moment, Jackie wondered where she would be able to hang it. What would she do with it after she left Paris? She knew explaining how this portrait came about would be difficult.

François could see that the experience of seeing her picture had begun to stir Jackie's passion. Because she had fastened all but the top two buttons on her blouse, the telltale signs of redness were displayed on her neck and the upper portion of her chest. As was often the case, she was not wearing a bra. François came over to the sofa and sat on the floor aside of Jackie. She was intently looking at her portrait, which she had propped up against a stool. François, ever so lightly, brushed his finger across Jackie's erect right breast. She made no attempt to restrain him and continued to peer at her likeness. He continued to caress her through the silk blouse, which produced a most sensuous feeling. He then turned to the left breast and rubbed the same way. Jackie looked down at him and said, "It looks like you know how to do more than just draw." He caressed the nape of her neck and began to kiss her. By this time, Jackie was becoming more than a little aroused. She returned his kisses and thrust her tongue into his open mouth. He responded in kind, and it was clear he was an experienced lover. In fact, François had made love to many young women and had far more experience than one would have expected of a man at twenty-nine years of age.

François was a lover who understood that men became aroused and moved to orgasm much faster than women. He was the type of lover that took the time to bring his partner along, He gently unbuttoned Jackie's blouse to reveal her breasts. It was all he could do when he drew Jackie's picture not to make love to her. By this time, Jackie decided to get involved, and it wasn't long before they were lost in giving each other the utmost pleasure. Jackie reached a level of satisfaction that night that was much better than any previous sexual encounter she had experienced. It was as if her previous lovers had been amateurs, and for the first time she made love with a man who knew what a woman wanted.

After they finished, they lay on the bed. Jackie pretended she had never used the bidet and asked François if he would show her how it worked. They went into the bathroom, and he proceeded to show Jackie how to operate it. She mounted it and began allowing the water to reach her innermost parts. Standing next to Jackie as he watched her on the bidet, François again became aroused. What followed was another explosion of passion that would remain in Jackie's memory for a long time.

After they finished making love, they got dressed and François drove Jackie back to her apartment with her portrait. Jackie had other lovers while in Paris, but none was the equal of François. She continued to see him until she left Paris at the end of the summer. Jackie learned a lot about herself that year. She got a great art education and learned what she wanted from sex. This experience would influence all her future relationships and prove to be one of the best times of her life.

4

Jackie and Jerry Meet

Soon after Jerry graduated from the Warton School in 1989, he rented an apartment in Princeton and commuted to his new job in New York. He was second in his class at Penn and landed a position with a most prestigious investment-banking firm on Wall Street. It was a real opportunity that didn't come to many and was the result of his hard work at college. Jerry was an athlete in college and tried to keep himself in shape by jogging. Despite his busy schedule, he was able to hit the trail one or two times during the week and every Saturday morning. His dedication paid off, and he was able to keep his build in spite of the business lunches and evening business meetings.

It was on one of his Saturday-morning runs that he first saw Jackie. She, too, kept her body in perfect shape by a combination of jogging and working out at the spa. It was in the spring of 1990 when Jerry looked up after completing his five-mile course to see this beautiful girl getting out of her car on her way to the running path. She saw Jerry about the same time he saw her. His six-foot-one-inch-tall athletic body glistened with sweat in the morning sun. He had a butt that caught Jackie's eye, and almost immediately there was an attraction between them.

Jackie walked to the path and said, "Hi. How was your run?"

"Great," he replied. "My name's Jerry French. What's yours?"

"Jackie. Jackie O'Donnell."

"Oh, that's why you have that red hair."

"You got it. Both my parents' families came from Ireland."

"Where in Ireland?"

"County Cork. Do you live around here?" Jackie asked. "I never saw you jogging before."

"Yes, I have an apartment in town. I was late today. Usually I run early on Saturday and finish before seven. However, I had a late night and overslept a bit. Do you live in Princeton?" Jerry asked.

"Yes, I still live at home with my parents. I'm an art teacher at an elementary school in Princeton. Do you work in the area, Jerry?"

"I work in New York, but I don't want to live there. I've gotten used to the ride in and out of the city, and it allows me to get some work done at the same time."

Jerry was about to say goodbye and head for his car, when he said, "How about dinner tonight?" Jackie didn't have anything planned, but was reluctant to let him know that. He sensed her hesitation and before she could answer, he said, "I guess that was a bit presumptuous of me. A girl that looks like you must have a full calendar."

Jackie responded, "Why don't you call me later." She gave Jerry her telephone number and they said goodbye.

Jerry didn't let any time pass before calling Jackie. In fact, he called her Sunday evening. Jackie's mother answered the phone, and Jerry said, "May I talk to Jackie?"

"Who is calling, please?"

"It's Jerry," was his reply.

Jackie sounded very friendly when she answered the phone. "Hi," she said. "Have you recovered from your jogging?"

"Yes. How was your weekend?"

"Busy. I can't believe it's Sunday night already."

"How would you like to go to dinner and a show next Saturday?" Jerry asked.

This time Jackie answered without delay: "Sure! Sounds like fun. What show did you have in mind?"

"Let that be a surprise," answered Jerry. "How about I pick you up at seven. That will give us time to get into the city for dinner by eight."

"OK, see you Saturday," Jackie replied.

The week flew by, and Jackie was looking forward to her first date with Jerry. She decided to go all out and wore a stunning midnight-blue dress that took every advantage of her outstanding figure. Jerry wondered what her body was like, since it wasn't easy to see it in the jogging suit she wore the week before. He felt sure, however, that because she worked out he would be pleased with what would greet him at seven o'clock.

To say Jerry was pleased was an understatement. He couldn't believe it when she opened the door. For a second he just stood there, but then caught himself from staring too long. "You look stunning! Your dress is beautiful," he said.

Likewise, Jackie was pleased when she saw him dressed in a suit. "Hi. Come in."

Jerry stepped into the entry room of the three-story colonial. The home was evidence that her family had money.

"Come and meet my parents," Jackie said. She introduced her parents to him, and they spent a few minutes getting acquainted.

A little after seven Jerry said, "I think we should get started." They said their goodbyes and headed for the train station.

"Do you use the train to go into New York?" he asked.

"Sometimes, but I don't get into the city very often," she replied.

Jerry had made dinner reservations at La Celebrities and had tickets for the Broadway show *Cats*. They both had a good time, and their date seemed to end all too soon. It was about 1:00 a.m. when they returned to Princeton, and Jerry drove her home from the train station.

When they arrived at her house she asked him, "Would you like to come in?"

"No, thank you. It's late and I wouldn't want to disturb your parents." He gave her a kiss good night, which she returned. As he turned to walk to his car, he said, "I'll call you this week. I had a great time."

"So did I," she replied.

Tuesday night Jerry called Jackie as he'd promised. "Do you like the Sixers?" he asked.

"Yes," she responded.

"I have tickets for the game Saturday night. Would you like to go?"

"Sure. That sounds like fun."

"We can have dinner at Bookbinders and then drive to the game."

Jackie dressed in a sporty outfit, and Jerry wore his Dockers. He picked her up about five o'clock, and they drove into Philadelphia.

The evening was mild and they had a good time. It was eleven thirty when they returned to Princeton. Jerry said, "How about a nightcap at my apartment?"

"OK. I would like to see your place."

As it turned out, Jerry's apartment was about fifteen minutes' drive from where Jackie lived. They went in, and Jerry asked Jackie if she would like some wine. They began a pleasant conversation, which led to an exchange of kisses that were very different from their first date. Jackie knew why she liked Jerry. He reminded her of François. Not by his appearance, but by his manner and the way he kissed. Before their two-hour nightcap was over, Jackie was sure that François and Jerry must have had the same lovemaking instructor. Jerry drove Jackie to her home, and they exchanged a kiss that said there would be many more.

From that second date, Jackie knew he was the one. Within a month, Jackie and Jerry were seeing each other on a regular basis, and they became engaged at Christmas that same year. The couple married the following June, and their wedding was the social event of the Princeton elite.

5

Jackie's Dream

When they reached their room, Jerry opened the door and carried Jackie in. He laid her on the bed and closed the door. Jackie watched with anticipation as he walked toward her. He said, "Let's continue what you started in the bar."

This was the beginning of a night that would fulfill Jackie's expectations. They began to kiss, and it didn't take long for Jerry's foreplay to bring Jackie's hot blood to a boil, and Jerry was able to bring her to the ultimate moment of pleasure. When they had finished, they sat by the fire and held each other.

This was something Jackie missed when they made love at home. Jerry eventually began to fall asleep, and Jackie said, "Let's go to bed. Maybe you can rise to the occasion in the morning."

"Never can tell," he replied.

"I love you," she said.

"I love you too."

They said good night and were soon asleep.

Not long after she fell asleep Jackie began dreaming. It was early August, and the weather was hot. Jackie was standing in her kitchen wearing a pair of white shorts, a T-shirt, and sandals. She was making potato salad for dinner when she heard a knock at the back door. It was the delivery boy with her groceries. She opened the door and said, "You must be new. I don't remember seeing you before."

"Yes, my name is Chris. I just started at the market last week."

"Do you live in the area?"

"Yes, I'm a student at Princeton. I took this job for a little spending money and because it fits into my schedule."

Jackie was having one of her horny days. She thought, *What a great-looking guy. My compliments to the grocery store manager for hiring such a hunk.* She watched him as he unloaded the groceries from his truck. She couldn't stop looking at him, especially his great buns. "It looks like you work out."

"Yes, I was a bodybuilder in high school. I still get to the gym, but my studies and this job make it hard to exercise as often as I would like."

Jackie asked, "Can you help me with the groceries?"

"Sure. I'll hand you the groceries and you can put them away." As he reached for a bag of jelly beans, it slipped out of his hand and broke all over the floor. "Sorry about that. Sometimes I'm a bit clumsy." Chris knelt down on the floor and began picking up the elusive beans.

Jackie moved next to him and pretended to work at the counter. It was clear she was flirting with this young man by the way she moved so close to him. Jackie looked down and said, "How are you doing?"

"Just fine, Mrs. French."

"Call me Jackie," she replied in a seductive voice.

Chris wondered what she really wanted. He decided to see just how far she was willing to go. He put his hand on her inner thigh and slid it up her leg to the edge of her shorts. Jackie continued to work at the counter, supposedly paying no attention to Chris. She didn't say anything, and Chris continued moving his hand under the leg of her shorts.

Jackie knew what she was doing was wrong. However, this forbidden touch felt so good, she didn't want to stop him. Part of her was aroused by the attention of this young stud, while another part wanted to stop. In the end, Jackie's passion won out, and their bodies became entangled in a burst of forbidden passion on the kitchen table on that hot, steamy August afternoon.

When Chris finished, he helped Jackie off the table and they got dressed. "I better get going. My boss will be looking for me," he said.

"You can tell him for me you did just fine!"

Jackie finished making the potato salad and decided to take a shower and change her clothes. She went up to the bathroom and took off her clothes. She turned the water on and stepped into the shower. The warm water felt good, and Jackie began to think about what she had done. She knew this would lead to trouble and vowed to never let it happen again. She finished her shower and got dressed just before Jerry came home with the kids. They had dinner, and Jackie tried to forget the afternoon.

That next week, Jackie did her best not to think of Chris or next week's grocery delivery. It was about two o'clock Saturday afternoon when Chris arrived with her order. She went to the door to let him in and said, "Put the bags on the counter." After Chris finished, Jackie said, "Let me get you a tip. I have my purse in the living room."

Chris wanted a repeat of last week and followed her into the living room. He came up behind her and began stroking the back of her neck. She said, "Please don't. Last week was a mistake. I'm married and can't get involved with you." Chris detected very little conviction in her voice and continued to caress her neck. His touch felt so good that she allowed him to continue. Chris unhooked Jackie's bra and began touching her until she responded by turning around and passionately kissing him. They fell to the floor, and before long they were again making love.

This second encounter was the beginning of a relationship that got hotter and hotter. It was hard for them to get enough of each other. The Saturday grocery delivery became an event Jackie planned for all week. She had to make sure that she was alone when Chris came. Their weekly rendezvous became a challenge to keep secret.

Mr. Jones, the store manager, started to receive complaints that Chris was late with his deliveries. When questioned, Chris denied he was late but said he would do his best to speed up his schedule. Despite their talk, the complaints continued. Mr. Jones decided to follow Chris the next Saturday to check on him. Chris had four orders for Saturday afternoon. He left the store about one o'clock with Mr. Jones following him in his car. The first delivery went to the Barrettes, who lived about four blocks from the Frenches. Chris pulled into the drive and unloaded the groceries. It took him about ten minutes, and he was on his way to the Frenches. Chris pulled into the drive, and Mr. Jones parked across the street to observe him. Jackie met him at the door, and he proceeded to unload her order.

Fifteen minutes turned into twenty and then to thirty minutes. Mr. Jones got out of his car and walked toward the house. He first looked in the delivery truck and saw the other two orders in the back awaiting delivery. He went to the back door. The curtain was pushed open, and he looked through the window and saw the groceries sitting on the counter in the kitchen. He couldn't see either Jackie or Chris. He decided to walk around to the front door and ring the bell. As he passed the living room window, he saw Jackie and Chris in what was obviously the last few minutes of their lovemaking. He could not believe it. Now it was clear why Chris was late for some of his deliveries each Saturday.

Mr. Jones decided not to get involved at that time and returned to his office. He told the cashier to send Chris to his office as soon as he returned from his deliveries. It was about three thirty when Chris returned. The cashier saw him come through the door and said, "You better get yourself to the boss's office! He wants to see you, and he didn't appear to be very happy about something." Chris ran up the stairs to Mr. Jones's second-floor office and knocked on the door.

"Come in."

"You wanted to see me."

"Sit down, Chris. I followed you this afternoon when you made your deliveries. I saw you and Mrs. French."

"I don't know what you mean."

"I saw you on the living room floor having sex with her. How long has this been going on?"

Chris knew it was useless to deny it and said, "About three months."

"Are you nuts? You have your whole life ahead of you. Why did you become involved with a married woman?"

"It just happened. I have no other answer for you." Chris asked, "Do you intend to tell Mr. French?"

"I don't know, but you are fired."

Chris got up and left his office. Dan Jones had known Jerry since he married Jackie, and they were good friends. He didn't want to become involved, but thought Jerry should know, especially since it was his delivery boy that was involved. He decided to call Jerry that evening. Dan told him he had something important to discuss with him and suggested they meet for breakfast the following Saturday. Jerry agreed, and they planned to meet at the local diner about eight o'clock.

Dan arrived first, and Jerry joined him just after eight.

"What's on your mind, Dan?" asked Jerry.

"This will be hard to tell you, Jerry. We've been friends for almost ten years."

"What in the world is bothering you?" said Jerry.

"I caught my delivery boy making love with Jackie."

"You're nuts. Why would Jackie do that?" Jerry asked.

"I don't know, Jerry, but I saw them on the floor of your living room going at it last Saturday."

"Why were you at my house?"

"Several customers had been complaining that my delivery boy Chris was late with his deliveries. This has been going on for several months, and I decided to follow him to see why he was running so late. After he spent over a half hour in your house, I went over to see if something was wrong. As I walked past your living room window on my way to the front door, I saw them," Dan explained.

Jerry turned bright red, got up from the table, and stormed out of the diner without saying a word.

It was at this point that Jackie woke up from her dream in a cold sweat. She was disoriented for a moment and tried to clear her head. *It must have been a dream,* she thought. Jackie got out of bed and went over to the sink for a drink of water. She could barely see herself in the mirror since it was just beginning to get light. She looked at the clock. It was a quarter to seven. Jackie wanted to wake Jerry and hold him. She somehow felt guilty for having such a dream. However, how would she explain waking him so early? She didn't want to tell him about her dream. She couldn't understand how it seemed so real.

Jackie returned to bed and tried to go back to sleep. She lay there unable to sleep until the clock read half past eight. At that point, she turned over and began to kiss Jerry. He finally awakened and said, "What time is it?"

"Time to begin where we left off last night," Jackie answered. She knew Jerry liked early-morning encounters, and she desperately wanted to forget her dream. Jackie thought what better way to forget than to make love with her husband. She decided to take charge of the lovemaking. From her earliest relationship with Rick, Jackie had a need to be in control of her life, especially when it came to sex. After their romantic beginning of the day, they took a shower together and went to breakfast.

6

A Saturday in the Poconos

Jerry responded, "It must be the early-morning exercise. Lucky for you they have a country breakfast."

"Well, maybe they know most of their guests like that same kind of activity in the morning."

"If that's the case, why isn't it listed on the activities sheet they gave us when we checked in?"

"Ha ha. You think you're funny," she quipped.

"Tomorrow they have a brunch starting at eleven o'clock, which will give us time for much more exercise," Jerry said.

"We'll see if you can keep up, my man. I know it won't be a problem for me," Jackie replied.

When they arrived at the dining room, the waiter asked them if they wanted to eat alone or be seated with another couple. Jerry said, "You may seat us with other guests." The waiter led them to a couple that looked to be in their late twenties.

"Hi. My name is Jerry French, and this is my wife, Jackie."

"Pleased to meet you. I'm Frank Schmidt and this is my girlfriend, Kathy Barber."

"Have you been here before, Frank?"

"No. This is our first time. How about you two?" Frank asked.

"This is our first visit as well."

"How did you find this place?" Frank asked.

Jackie piped in, "This was my plan. We needed to get away from the routine, the kids, and the job for a short time. I found the inn on the internet."

Frank responded, "You won't believe this, but I designed their web page at my company in Philadelphia. That's why we are here. The inn asked us to spend a weekend on them because they received so many hits on their website."

"You really did a great job. It was the cleverness of the web page that made me call and get a reservation," Jackie said.

"Hey, tell the manager," responded Frank. "Maybe they'll give us another freebie. Where do you live?"

"We live in Princeton," Jerry replied.

"That's an expensive area. I hear a lot of big shots from New York live there. Where do you work, Jerry?"

"Wall Street."

"Oops! Looks like I put my foot in my mouth," Frank said.

Kathy tried to smooth things over. "Frank isn't critical about people who work in the big city, it's just his way."

"No offense taken," Jerry replied.

"What do you plan on doing today?" Jackie asked.

"Oh, I think we'll look around this morning and spend some time in the hot tub this afternoon. What do you two have planned?" Kathy asked.

Jackie responded, "See the sights. There seems to be so much to do in this area."

The waiter arrived with coffee and took their order. They had a delicious breakfast and enjoyed their conversation. After they finished, Jackie said, "How about having dinner together?"

Kathy answered, "That sounds great. What time do you want to meet?"

"How does eight sound?"

"Fine. See you then. Have a fun day."

As they were walking through the lobby, Jackie spotted a rack that held scores of brochures and maps of the area. "Let's stop and see where we want to go," she said.

"Why don't you see if they have something about the candy factory you wanted to visit," Jerry said. They began to look over the rack and took some brochures. Jackie found an area map that identified the local attractions. "Here's something about the candy factory. It's near a place called Cresco on Route Three Ninety," Jerry said. Now all we have to do is find Route Three Ninety."

"Let's take all this stuff to our room and plan where we want to go," Jackie said.

When they got to the room, the maid was just finishing cleaning. When she saw them, she hurriedly completed her work. Jerry said, "Maybe she thinks you look horny and need some attention." Although that thought had not crossed Jackie's mind, the suggestion did give her a little shot of adrenaline.

She pulled Jerry into the room and closed the door. "Let's see if your friend is interested." It didn't take Jackie long to gain Jerry's attention, and what followed was a brief but passionate lovemaking session.

"Well, that makes the effort of the maid justified," Jackie pointed out.

Jerry got dressed and Jackie used the bathroom. They decided to drive to the candy factory. The map indicated a Christmas shop and an antique store on the way. Jackie said, "We may stop at a few places before we get to the candy factory." They gathered up their things and walked to the car.

When they got outside, they saw it had snowed about eight inches during the night. Jerry said, "I wonder if they've plowed the roads yet."

"Do you think we'll have a problem?" Jackie asked.

No, the SUV will do just fine." They had purchased a new Lincoln SUV in the fall, and this would be the first time Jerry would have a chance to try the four-wheel drive.

They had been on the road a short time when they saw a sign for Route 940. Jackie was the navigator and said, "We want to go east on Nine Forty." Almost immediately Jackie spotted the 940 sign and Jerry turned east. "Now we need to find Three Ninety. The town of Cresco is where we want to end up."

They had been on 940 for five minutes when they saw the Christmas shop. "Turn in!"

"Don't we have enough decorations?" Jerry asked.

"You can never get enough Christmas," Jackie responded.

"Fine. I'll pull in so you can find some more treasures." They spent a short time looking around, and Jackie managed to buy only one basket of decorations. Jerry paid the clerk, and they were back on the road again. "The sign indicates it's five miles to Three Ninety. You'll want to go north on Three Ninety." It wasn't long before they arrived at the candy factory.

The sign outside listed times when there was a demonstration showing how they made their candy. It was 11:20 a.m., and Jackie exclaimed, "Great! We arrived just in time. There's a demonstration as eleven thirty." They parked and went into the building. On the right side was a never-ending display of just about any type of candy one had ever seen. To the left of the front door was a seating area. People were starting to take their seats, and Jackie said, "Let's sit near the front."

It wasn't long before the owner came out of the kitchen to begin the demonstration. He explained how various types of candy were made and a little about his establishment. He worked as he spoke and was both informative and entertaining.

It was clear he had a bit of the actor in him. He explained that they made new items all the time and often used popular issues for new candy shapes. One person asked if he made a Monica sucker. He said, "As a matter of fact, you will find several Clinton-related items in the showroom." His demonstration took about twenty minutes, and everyone seemed to enjoy it. At the end of his talk, he told the audience of another enterprise his family owned in the area: a pretzel bakery where you could twist your own pretzel and they would bake it for you. Jackie and Jerry selected candy for themselves and some to take home as gifts. They decided to look for the pretzel bakery and drove off in the direction outlined on yet another brochure.

By the time they decided to head back to the inn, in addition to their earlier stops, they had been to a cider press, an antique store, a candle factory and a stained-glass shop. Jackie also wanted to stop at a leather and boot shop they saw just before they got back to the inn. Jerry said, "Why don't we stop there tomorrow on the way home."

"That sounds fine," she agreed, and they soon found the small road that led to the inn. It was about six o'clock when they pulled into the parking lot. They locked the car, with all their treasures from the day inside, and went to their room.

Jackie decided she wanted to take a shower before dinner, and Jerry walked to the bar. He saw Frank watching ice hockey and decided to join him.

"Did you have a good day?" Frank asked.

"Yes. How about you?"

"We had a very relaxing day. The hot tub is great. I'd like to get one sometime." They had a few drinks and waited for the girls to join them.

It was seven thirty when Jackie came into the bar, and a few minutes later Kathy arrived. They ordered a round of drinks and began to talk about what they had done since breakfast. All agreed their first day at the Inn of Destiny had been fun. A little after eight, they decided to go to the dining room. The waiter seated them near the fireplace with the now familiar soup pots simmering over the fire. They were all hungry since they hadn't taken the time for lunch.

They took a few minutes going over the menu, and when the waiter saw that they looked ready to order he came to the table. Jackie decided to try the shrimp since she had a steak on Friday evening. Kathy wanted pasta and ordered the homemade ravioli. Both men decided on beef. Jerry had a porterhouse, and Frank a New York strip. They had an enjoyable meal and decided to return to the bar for an after-dinner drink.

The inn had a comedian, who turned out to be quite good. Most of his humor was a bit off-color, but, after all, there were no children present. When he finished his act, the combo began to play. The couples listened to the music until half past twelve and then said good night. As they walked to their room Jerry wondered if Jackie had more romance in mind. They had not made love this often since their honeymoon.

7

Jerry's Dream

As they were returning to room D, Jerry decided he would take charge of the lovemaking tonight. After all, it had been Jackie's show that morning, and he wanted to give her pleasure tonight. Jerry had visited one of those specialty shops in the mall before their trip and picked up some love lotion. He selected strawberry to flavor Jackie's female parts. He hadn't said anything about his purchase and thought Saturday night would be the right time to try this stuff out. Jackie had kidded about it when she saw the lotion in the store but had never purchased any.

Jackie had also been to the mall to visit Jerry's favorite store, Victoria's Secret. She purchased a set consisting of a white camisole and micropanties. It's doubtful there was a square yard of cloth in the entire outfit. When they reached their room, Jackie took a bag from the drawer and headed to the bathroom. "I'll be right out." Jerry wanted to know what was in the little bag. Jackie replied, "Just wait and see. I think you'll approve."

In the meantime, Jerry changed into his silk PJ bottoms and lit the fire. He opened a bottle of wine, turned off the lights, and lit the oil lamp on the dresser. The combination of the fire and the oil lamp cast a romantic setting for Jackie's entrance. Jerry took one look at Jackie's surprise mall purchase and said, "Wow! Where did you get that?"

"I went to your favorite store in the mall, Victoria's Secret."

Jerry said, "You look better than any of their models!"

"Well, you should know; you look at them every time we pass it. Maybe I should see if they would hire me as one of their models," Jackie suggested.

"I don't think so. You may only model for me," Jerry replied.

Jackie's most sensuous female assets were her breasts. It was as if her nipples wanted to break free from whatever covered them. When Jerry saw men staring at her chest, he would first want them to stop while also liking it because he knew they envied him. Jackie came over to Jerry and sat by the fireplace. She picked up her glass of wine and offered a toast: "To a great weekend!"

"And there's more to come!" Jerry responded.

They began to kiss. Jackie put her finger into the wine and rubbed it on Jerry's lips. Jerry got out the bottle of love lotion and said, "I got this to rub on certain parts of you."

"You didn't. When did you get that?"

"Well, I shop at the mall too," was his response. Jerry removed her camisole so he could apply the lotion to her breasts. He poured the red fluid on his fingers and rubbed it over her breasts. It felt good to Jackie, and she watched him as his pleasure grew with each drop. After he had applied a liberal amount of the sweet, sticky fluid, he started to gently lick it off. Jackie didn't know if it felt better when Jerry put it on or licked it off. Jerry said, "This tastes good. I'm glad I got the strawberry-flavored lotion." He made several applications, reveling in the process each time. He then began to apply the lotion to her tummy and navel. Just as before, licking it off proved to be best.

Jerry removed her micropanties so that he didn't stain them with strawberry lotion. First, he went down to her feet and put it between her toes. He licked them clean, which drove Jackie almost to the edge. She loved to have her feet rubbed, but licking between her toes was almost more than she could stand. It was time for the pièce de résistance. Jerry stuck his finger in the bottle and began applying the lotion to her most sacred parts.

"That feels so good," she moaned.

"Wait until I remove it," Jerry said. By the time Jerry had finished with the love lotion, Jackie was to the point of no return, and Jerry proceeded to complete his performance. When they both finished, Jackie and Jerry lay on the floor for some time, their naked bodies melding as one. When they had finished, Jackie washed herself off and they got into bed. They decided to sleep in the nude and agreed to begin again whenever the urge came to either of them during the night. It wasn't long before they fell asleep in each other's arms.

Jerry began to dream with the sounds of the commuter train rumbling in his head. He was looking out the window of the train, watching the familiar scenery streak past. He opened the *Journal* and began reading. He liked his train ride and used the time to catch up on the news or do some reading for work. As he pored over the financial news, Jerry spotted an article recapping the past six months of a new company his broker had tried to get him to purchase. Jerry's firm purchased and operated commercial properties, such as large shopping centers and major office complexes. He was the person who negotiated most of the purchase agreements.

His deals had proven to be so successful that when his boss was promoted to CEO, Jerry took his position as head of acquisitions. Along with Jerry's new job was a very sizable increase in salary, a larger share of the profits via stock options, and the title senior VP. Jerry was always on the lookout for investment opportunities. Although he had large holdings in his firm, he wanted to take advantage of other lucrative opportunities as well.

Jerry's Warton classmate and friend David Strong was a broker on Wall Street. One of his specialties was new public offerings, known in the trade as IPOs. Dave regularly called Jerry and kept him informed of the latest IPOs that looked promising. Jerry at times was hesitant, as was the case six months ago with the new company he was reading about. Dave had tried to convince Jerry to purchase a few thousand shares, but to no avail. The bottom line was, Jerry screwed up. The company took off and was up sevenfold in six months. In addition, its growth didn't falter, as was often the case with new offerings.

When Jerry arrived at his office, there was a call from Dave. "I have a hot new stock for you! This is better than the one you missed in November. Did you read the article about it in the *Journal?*"

"Yes, I saw it. You were right, I should have jumped in on that company," Jerry replied.

Dave proceeded to review Surgical Ventures with Jerry. This was a new firm that had developed the formula used for surgical glue. This material was akin to superglue but was used in place of stitches for certain applications.

This material could be used on most cuts that didn't exceed five inches in length and didn't involve any sizable blood vessels. It was so simple that it had great potential. Not only was it painless and assisted in fighting germs, the material was eventually absorbed into the skin and there was no need to have the stitches removed.

Dave said, "It's only a matter of time and this company will be purchased by one of the large pharmaceutical companies. When that happens, the initial investors should make a killing!"

"Send me the prospectus and I will call you," Jerry responded.

"You don't have much time. I think I can get my hands on about five thousand shares for you if you are interested. The initial price is expected to be ten dollars per share," Dave explained.

"OK. I will call you," Jerry said, and hung up.

On Monday Jerry placed an order for the five thousand shares. Four months later, the price shot up to eighty dollars per share on the word that a large drug company was interested in purchasing the company. Jerry sold his shares and made over $300,000 with a $50,000 investment.

All of a sudden, the feel of Jackie's hand awakened Jerry. After a few minutes, she went under the covers to make sure Jerry was ready for her. She climbed on top and started to kiss Jerry. It didn't take Jackie long to show who was the boss, as Jerry soon experienced another explosion. When he finished, Jackie hopped off and headed for the bathroom. Jackie returned to bed, and they were both soon fast asleep.

When Jerry started to dream again it was December and the first snow of the season had just started to fall. He was watching it through his thirtieth-floor office windows when the telephone rang. It was Dave with another IPO for Jerry. "I have the best one yet," said Dave.

"You say that every time, Dave," Jerry responded.

"Do I have to remind you about the three hundred grand you made on the last stock?"

"No, I remember," Jerry answered.

"The company name is Optiscan," said Dave. "It expects to go public next week." He explained the company had developed a system that made positive identification by scanning the iris of the eye.

"That sounds similar to fingerprint ID systems."

"Yes, only far better." Dave explained how the system worked. "The user stands from one to three feet from the cameras used for scanning. The actual scan takes about two seconds, and within another two seconds, the identification is complete. The first camera scans the person's face to establish the location of the eyes. The second camera zooms in on the eye to capture the digital image.

"The system uses a circular grid as a guide to develop the pattern in the iris. Every person has a different pattern, just like everyone has unique fingerprints. The grid is overlaid, and the light and dark areas are converted to a human bar code. It's this bar code that's used by the computer system to make the identification with the master records, which are stored in a secure database. The system uses available light, which eliminates any potential damage to the eye. It scans through eyeglasses and contact lenses. The potential applications for this system are enormous. The first group that's talking with Optiscan is the companies that make ATM machines. Security companies, governmental agencies, and anyone that needs positive ID are potential users. This could also replace time clocks. So, what do you think?" Dave asked.

"It does sound like the best one yet, my friend. How many shares do you think you can get and at what price?"

"I know I can get you ten thousand shares. I expect the initial price to be fifteen dollars per share."

"Great. Fax the prospectus over, and I'll call you later this afternoon," Jerry replied. They said goodbye and hung up.

Jerry told his assistant to bring him the fax just as soon as it arrived. In about ten minutes, the fax was on his desk. After Jerry read it, he picked up the phone to call Dave. His line was busy and the receptionist answered the call. "Do you want to hold, or shall I have Mr. Strong call you back?"

"I'll wait," Jerry responded.

In a few minutes Dave picked up and said, "Jerry, I can get you twelve thousand at fifteen dollars per share."

"That would be a hundred and eighty grand," Jerry responded. "That may be a little more than I want to risk."

"Did you forget the three-hundred-thousand-dollar profit you made on Surgical Ventures?"

"No, I remember. Go ahead and buy me the twelve thousand shares."

"I'll call you when the deal is done. Better get your money ready," Dave added.

"Fine," Jerry replied. They hung up, and Jerry went back to a potential acquisition he was reviewing.

It was Thursday when Dave called to tell Jerry that he was the owner of twelve thousand shares of Optiscan. During the next three months, the stock took off, and by the end of March it was selling for eighty-eight dollars per share. Jerry decided to take a quick profit and told Dave to sell his twelve thousand shares. In a little over ninety days, Jerry had made almost three-quarters of a million dollars on Optiscan.

Before Jerry knew it, his dream had shifted to the spring. It was April 14, just two days before the tax deadline. It was a pleasant day, and he was on the golf course with his boss, Barry Hagman. They were about to tee off on the seventh hole when both their cell phones started to ring.

"That's odd! Both phones ringing at the same time," Jerry remarked. As it turned out, both calls were coming from different people at their office. They were informed there was a very sharp sell-off on the market that was precipitated by a potentially catastrophic problem in the Middle East. After they completed their calls, they decided to cut short their golf game and return to the office.

By the time they arrived on the thirtieth floor, the Dow was down almost a thousand points, and the losers versus winners showed a margin of twenty to one. The problem resulted from a serious impasse between the Israelis and Palestinians over the final peace agreement. Israel refused any settlement that changed the status of Jerusalem or ended their West Bank settlements. The Palestinians insisted there be international sharing of the city as part of the final peace agreement, as well as the end of the Israeli settlements in the West Bank. For almost eighteen months, the discussions had been underway with no settlement. In a last attempt to pressure the Israelis, the Palestinians convinced the moderate Arab coalition to back their demand for some change to the status of Jerusalem. When this didn't produce the desired outcome, the Arab oil cartel threatened to withhold oil from the West until Israel changed its position.

That brought the direst problem for the United States as well as the rest of the Western alliance. On one hand, Israel considered Jerusalem like the US considered Washington, D.C., and no amount of pressure from the US was likely to alter their opposition. On the other hand, establishing who had ownership rights to most areas in this part of the world was impossible. The history of ownership depended on the date one chose. The other reality was that Western economies couldn't operate without oil from the Middle East.

This situation might be viewed by the radical factions in the Middle East as an opportunity to grab more power or territory. It had the real potential to create uncontrollable economic and military issues. The White House was in crisis mode desperately trying to find a solution to the impasse. The president put the military on alert and moved two more navy battle groups within striking distance of the Middle East. He wanted to show that the US wouldn't allow any of the factions to take military advantage of the situation.

Jerry decided he had better stay in New York to follow the situation. He was heavily invested in the market with small-cap and international stocks that he owned outright as well as a number of stocks he'd purchased on margin. The margin calls had already taken more than half his liquid funds. He called Jackie to explain the situation and to tell her he wouldn't be home Thursday night.

By the close of the market, the Dow had lost twenty-five hundred points and Jerry had lost 30 percent of his net worth in securities. To sell now would be a catastrophic loss. On the other hand, what would tomorrow bring? Friday, the market opened on the down side. By eleven o'clock, there was a story that the president may have been able to get some movement. By noon, it was clear that this wasn't the case and the Dow fell another three thousand points. The losses were so widespread that the decision was made to suspend trading at 2:00 p.m. By this time, Jerry had suffered a 75 percent decline in the value of his portfolio because he was concentrated in companies that were impacted to a greater extent than the market overall. In addition, he was unable to cover the last margin call and was sold out on the stocks he had purchased on credit. Jerry didn't know what to do. If only he had gotten out when they first returned to the office yesterday, his losses would be only one-third as great.

Jerry was so upset by his dream that it awakened him and he found himself in a cold sweat. He was relieved when he discovered it was all a dream. It seemed so real. All his dreams that night seemed as though the events had already taken place. Jerry got up and washed his face, as if to make sure this was just a bad dream!

8

Sunday Morning at the Inn

It was early when Jerry finished in the bathroom, and he returned to bed. He gazed at Jackie peacefully sleeping and thought how beautiful she was lying there. She looked so serene, and he didn't want to disturb her. He carefully slipped into bed and went back to sleep. It seemed like only a few minutes since Jerry had woken from his dream when he felt Jackie begin to stir.

"Are you awake, dear?" Jerry asked.

"I think so. What time is it?" she asked.

Jerry looked at the alarm clock on the nightstand and to his surprise it read 9:15 a.m. "You won't believe it! It's after nine," he responded.

"How did it get that late?" Jackie asked.

"I guess it must have been all the activity this weekend."

Jackie got out of bed and walked over to the mirror at the sink. "I look a wreck!"

"You are beautiful. In fact, you look better first thing in the morning than other women look anytime during the day," Jerry said.

That made Jackie feel good. She knew that she was attractive, but it was important for her to know that Jerry thought so too. The prospect of getting older was beginning to creep into Jackie's thoughts, and she wondered when her body would begin to show reality. For now, she was able to convince herself that medical science would eventually find the "fountain of youth." After all, there was a lot of research being done on the aging process. Whoever unlocked the secret of youth would definitely reap a gigantic prize.

Jackie went into the bathroom and turned on the shower. She stepped into the tub and pulled the curtain closed. The warm water felt good as it cascaded down her exquisite body. This feeling awakened the memory of her dream from Friday night of her affair with Chris. Even though it was just a dream, the memory seemed so real to Jackie. She relived the opposing emotions she'd experienced: guilt and lust.

Her thoughts were interrupted as she saw the shower curtain slide open and Jerry stepped in.

"Need some help?" he asked.

"I can always use your help," she responded.

Jerry took the soft nylon puff from her hand and squirted a liberal amount of strawberry-scented bath gel on it from the dispenser mounted on the shower wall. As he began to gently rub the gel over Jackie's back, that distinctive aroma filled her nostrils. She was immediately taken back to last night's lovemaking. Jerry had given her a most pleasurable experience that would remain in her memory for a long time.

"That feels good!" she exclaimed. "Don't stop with my back!"

Jerry didn't intend to neglect any part of her. When he had thoroughly washed Jackie's back, he moved down a bit to her buttocks and the backs of her legs. He turned her to the front and completed the job, paying special attention to her breasts and her voluminous red patch, which had fully recovered from the bikini trim of last summer. By the time Jerry completed his job, Jackie was clean enough to perform surgery. In addition, he was again ready for action, even though Jackie hadn't assisted in the process other than allowing him to wash her body. He began to kiss her under the falling water of the shower, and their tongues quickly began a dueling contest. Nothing turned Jackie on faster than French kissing. Her experience with François must have been partly responsible. Jackie reached for the bath-gel dispenser and took some of the magical fluid and applied it to the proper part of Jerry.

"You are the best lover I ever had!" Jerry declared.

"And how many are you comparing it to?" Jackie questioned.

"None of your business. All you have to know is it's been the only one since our second date."

"Well, what about between our first and second dates?" she asked.

"I'm not talking," he responded.

"Oh, you were messing around after you met me." Before Jerry could respond, Jackie began to think of her past, especially the year in Paris, and decided to drop the subject. "Never mind. As long as you didn't have anyone after you had me, that's fine."

Jerry liked shower sex, and this standing position enabled him to control the action and last longer. After almost a half hour, Jackie was impressed. "That's the longest you ever lasted. It must be all that sex you had over the weekend," she reminded him. Jerry just grinned, as he, too, was pleased with his performance that weekend.

They finished their shower and got dressed. By this time, it was after eleven o'clock. Jackie decided to pack their suitcases before they went down for brunch. The checkout time was 12:30 p.m., and she thought it would be better to be packed so they could leave after they ate. They walked to the dining room holding hands.

As they passed the registration desk, Jerry saw it was slow and decided to check out except for turning in the key. The desk clerk asked them, "How did you enjoy your stay with us?"

"We had a very good time," Jerry responded.

The clerk entered their name into the computer and said, "Oh, you were in room D I see." Jerry wondered why he made mention of the fact they were in room D.

After the clerk ran Jerry's credit card through the system, it printed out a receipt. At the very bottom of the receipt was the following message: *We at the Inn of Destiny are pleased you spent the weekend with us and hope all your dreams come true. The Management.*

When Jackie and Jerry arrived at the dining room, they spotted Frank and Kathy, who had just been seated. They beckoned them to come over and join them. "Hi! Please have brunch with us," Kathy said.

"Great! We would love to," Jackie responded.

"Did you check out?" Jerry asked.

"Yes, we did," Frank responded. "We need to get on the road as soon as brunch is over. I have some work on a new website. The client wants to see it first thing Monday morning."

"Did you have to go through the normal checkout procedure since you were on a freebie?" Jerry asked.

"Yes, all they did was enter a credit for the cost of the weekend. They do that for tax purposes."

Frank showed it to Jerry, who said, "That's what I call a great rate. You can't beat zero." As Jerry glanced at Frank's receipt, he noticed the message on the bottom was slightly different. It said, *We at The Inn of Destiny are pleased you spent the weekend with us and hope you had a good time. Please come back soon. The Management.* Jerry wondered why there would be a different message on his receipt. He didn't comment, however, and handed it back to Frank.

The two couples proceeded to the extensive array of food that the inn provided for this parting amenity. Like everything else at the inn, the brunch was outstanding both in the selection and quality of the cuisine. When they finished, the two couples thanked each other for their company and exchanged phone numbers.

"We must get together. Princeton and Philadelphia are close," Frank said.

"Sounds great! We will call you," Jackie replied. They shook hands and left the dining room. Jackie and Jerry made one last visit to their room to use the bathroom and make sure they didn't leave anything behind. They'd had a fantastic weekend. The Inn of Destiny had lived up to the claims on its web page. What they didn't know was that their adventure at the inn wasn't over.

9

Return to Princeton

As Jerry and Jackie were leaving the inn, they noticed a billboard advertising a large flea market on Route 209. Jackie said, "Do we have time to stop and do some shopping?"

"I guess so. We told your parents we would pick the kids up at dinnertime," Jerry answered.

They had been on the road about twenty minutes when Jackie saw a sign for Route 209. "You go south, and we should see signs for the flea market soon after we turn onto Two Oh Nine." As advertised, the flea market was on the left, and Jerry pulled into the field that was used as a parking lot. Though it was frozen, Jerry commented, "I bet this field is a problem if they get too much rain during the spring or summer."

"This place is huge," Jackie commented. She was right. There were dozens of interlocking buildings and several hundred vendors. This was advertised as one of the largest flea markets in the area. They had merchants selling almost anything one could imagine. When Jackie saw the extent of the place, she shifted into shopping mode. Jerry was not as enthusiastic until he discovered an antique dealer that specialized in Civil War items. Other than golf, this was one of Jerry's few hobbies, and he couldn't believe his luck.

Jerry was a bit of an expert on the Civil War. He first asked to examine some of the items the dealer had for sale to see if they were fakes. After examining several pieces, he was convinced the items were genuine. "Would you believe I would find this in the Poconos?" he said to Jackie. Jerry spent about a half hour looking over the supply of artifacts and purchased a set of buttons from a Confederate officer's uniform. He also looked at a few old pictures that were said to have been taken by Brady, the famous Civil War photographer. However, Jerry was not 100 percent sure they were actually taken by Brady and decided to pass. They spent several hours and got things for the folks at home. Jackie purchased a Poconos T-shirt and an apple-paring machine.

"We better get on the road. It will take us until five o'clock even with light traffic," Jerry said. "Why don't you call your parents and tell them to expect us between five and five thirty. Ask them if we should pick up pizza and bring it with us. We can all eat together at their house and then drive home and get the kids settled for the night."

"Sounds good. I'll see if that's OK with my parents." Jackie called them on the phone, and they agreed pizza was a good idea.

It was just after five o'clock when they arrived at Jackie's parents' home in Princeton. The kids ran out to greet them. It was great to get away, but they were glad to see the children and her parents.

"Let's get the pizza out before it gets cold," Jerry said. They had called ahead when they were twenty minutes from the pizza place.

As they ate, Jackie gave them a thumbnail sketch of the inn. She also said they had surprises for everyone in the car. Lisa wanted to know what they had brought for them. "Just be patient. You will see soon enough," Jackie said. After they finished the pizza, Jerry went to the car and brought in the bags with their flea market purchases.

Lisa and David each got a new video game for their PlayStation. It proved a mistake to give the kids their presents first. All they wanted to do was go home to try their new games. For Jackie's father they got a DVD of the movie *Titanic*. Jackie's mother got a new gourmet cookbook. This was just the thing for her because Jackie's parents belonged to a gourmet group. They would have parties and try out the latest culinary delights.

After everyone had opened their gifts, Jackie and Jerry loaded the kids and their suitcase in the SUV and started the drive home. It was dark when they pulled into their driveway, and the kids couldn't wait to play the video games. "You must first get your bath; then you can play for a short time before bed," Jackie told them.

"Do we have to get a bath first?" David asked.

"Yes, no arguments," Jackie responded.

They dashed up the stairs, and David took his bath first. Jackie helped Lisa with her bath, and they went to the playroom and tried out their new games. Jackie allowed them to stay up a half hour past their normal bedtime. She knew they were excited.

At nine o'clock, Jackie said, "Time for bed, kids." They turned off the game and went to their bedrooms. As Jackie tucked them in, Jerry put the car in the garage. When he came back into the house, he came to their room and said good night to them. He then told Jackie he had to get things ready for a Monday-morning meeting and took his briefcase into the study.

Jackie took the empty suitcases to the attic. She had a hard time even getting into it since everything was piled at the top of the pull-down steps. She decided to rearrange a few things in the attic to make it easier to replace the suitcases. As Jackie was moving things around, she spotted an old wardrobe in one corner. She unzipped it and saw it was full of her old clothes. Some of them went back to her days at Smith. She took several items out and tried to remember the last time she wore each one. In the bottom of the wardrobe was a shipping tube. She pulled it out and removed one end cap. There was a rolled-up piece of paper in the tube. Jackie removed it and began to unroll it. It was the nude portrait François had drawn in Paris. She had forgotten how great the drawing was and how beautiful and happy she looked in the picture.

Suddenly she heard Jerry calling, "Jackie, where are you?"

"I'm in the attic putting the suitcases away."

"You didn't have to do that. I would have put them away," he replied.

"It was no problem; they're light. I'll be down in a second." Jackie quickly put the drawing back in the tube and placed it in the wardrobe. Now was not the time to dig into the past. In fact, she didn't intend to show her portrait to Jerry.

She climbed down the ladder and turned the attic light off. Jerry had come up to help her and pushed the spring-loaded access door into place. "Did you say good night to the kids?" Jackie asked.

"Yes. They're all set for the night. They wanted to play longer with their new video games. I told them maybe tomorrow. I think they spend too much time playing those games," Jerry said.

"Well, I know how engrossed I can become at the computer at times," Jackie responded.

"You seemed to be able to keep yourself occupied this weekend without the computer," Jerry quipped.

"Ha ha. You think you are funny," Jackie responded.

They went into the family room to relax after their weekend adventure. They held each other on the sofa and began to kiss. This time their kissing was not a prelude to something else but just to be with each other after a most enjoyable time together. As they relaxed, Jerry told her how glad he was that she had arranged their weekend at the inn. Jackie had hoped for a romantic interlude, and it was that and more. Jerry loved Jackie, but he didn't seem to realize that Jackie's physical needs weren't being fully met at times. Jackie and Mary often discussed her need for sex and how she should communicate this to Jerry. Jackie wasn't shy, but she didn't want Jerry to feel inadequate by her becoming too forward. Jerry enjoyed sex, too, and never strayed from his marriage vows. Jackie needed to find a way of making Jerry aware of her needs. At times, she felt close to exploding with pent-up up sexual desire. She knew the answer was not to go away each weekend and hoped their trip had reminded Jerry how good sex could be with her. *Maybe this will spark him into action more often*, Jackie thought.

Jerry was thinking of how great the sex had been that weekend and was proud of himself. *I still have it,* he thought. *I was able to keep up with Jackie.* He wondered what was up with her. She had never wanted so much sex since their honeymoon.

It was almost eleven o'clock when they decided to take a shower together and have one last interlude to cap off the weekend. After their lovemaking in the shower, they got dressed for bed and said good night. Before Jackie fell asleep, Jerry turned to her and said, "I love you, Jackie."

"I love you too," she responded.

10

Back to Normal

IT WAS BACK TO NORMAL for Jackie, as the alarm clock let her know it was six o'clock and time to get up. She rolled out and put her robe on to help shield her from the cold winter morning. She could hear the heater trying to get ahead of the night setting and bring the house to a comfortable state. Ice had formed along the edges of the windows, indicating how cold it was this February morning. Jackie's weekday routine found her making sure Jerry and the kids were awake, and starting breakfast.

Jerry went directly to the shower and then ate breakfast with the kids and Jackie. They tried to eat breakfast during the week as a family. Given the fast pace of the rest of their lives, both Jackie and Jerry felt that having breakfast together was important. Jerry had to be at the train station to get the 7:20, which required him to be out of the house by seven.

Today the kids lingered a bit and Jackie had to call them a second time. "You better get up," she said sternly. That brought the sound of little feet on the stairs, and Lisa and David appeared at the kitchen doorway.

"Sit down. What do you want this morning?" Jackie inquired. Lisa decided on Frosted Flakes and David wanted a scrambled egg. A few minutes later Jerry came into the kitchen and asked Jackie to adjust his tie. He had some toast, juice, and several cups of coffee. Jerry was also a bit slow this morning and looked at his watch to see it was already several minutes past seven. "I'm late." He grabbed his hat, coat, and briefcase as he kissed the kids and gave Jackie a passing kiss as he ran out the door. She knew he was a bit late but had hoped for a kiss more reflective of their weekend. She thought, *I guess the weekend is really over!*

She got the kids to finish their breakfast and brush their teeth. "Bundle up. It's very cold and windy out this morning." Jackie always walked to the sidewalk and watched them until they got to the bus stop. There were several other kids there, and Jackie waited until the bus picked them up before returning to the kitchen. She wanted to quickly clean up the breakfast dishes, knowing Mary would be coming soon to get the skinny on her weekend.

It was just before eight o'clock when Jackie heard Mary's familiar voice calling to her. "Hi! Let me see if you have a big smile on your face," she said.

"Sex—is that all you think about?" Jackie asked.

"*Me?* You should talk. The last thing you showed me before you left Friday was the sexy white number you got at Victoria's Secret."

Jackie asked Mary if she wanted some coffee, which was one of those non-questions. Mary always had coffee with Jackie, either at Jackie's or at her place. Jackie and Mary shared almost everything together, just like Jackie had with Barb when she was in college.

"Come on, give. Tell me everything," Mary demanded.

Jackie described the trip to the Poconos and the way the inn looked. "It was just like the material I showed you from the internet," she said. She explained the blending of old and new and the friendly reception as they had checked in. "They asked us to sign in using a quill pen and then proceeded to complete our registration on the computer. John would have been impressed with the construction of the inn. Jerry said he didn't think they used any nails. It was constructed using handmade joints and wooden pegs."

"Did Jerry approve of your choice?" Mary asked.

"Yes. I know he had good time. He didn't mention work one time. I made damn sure of that," Jackie remarked.

"What did you do after checking in to your room?" Mary wanted to know.

"We unpacked and Jerry went to the bar. This gave me a chance to use the whirlpool tub and prepare for my first surprise."

"What do you mean, 'surprise'?" Mary asked.

Jackie answered, "Well, when I got dressed I didn't put on any bra or panties. In addition, I wore my western outfit with the short skirt. I completed the outfit with that wide belt and my boots. I was hot, both on the outside and underneath."

"Did Jerry know you weren't wearing underclothing?"

"Well, parts of the dining room were a bit chilly, which made my nipples get hard. I knew he saw them although he didn't say anything. He did rub against me a lot when we were dancing after dinner," Jackie said. She explained how she had sat on the barstool and parted her legs so Jerry would see she wasn't wearing panties.

"Weren't you afraid some of the other men would see you?" Mary asked.

"Well, I was careful. Besides, by that time I didn't mind if a few saw my show. After all, I'll never see them again, and it may have gotten them ready for their after-dinner activities. Who knows?" Jackie responded.

"What happened after that?" Mary questioned.

Jackie gave her a general idea about the remainder of the evening. "Jerry is a great lover when he wants to be. He reminds me of François," she explained. She had told Mary a little about her year in Paris but had never gone into the details of her relationship with François.

"Tell me more about François. It sounds like he was much more than just a casual acquaintance," Mary demanded.

"François was the best lover I ever had," Jackie admitted.

"Come on. Give me all the details. How did you meet him? What did you do together?" Mary asked. She was getting excited just wondering what her friend had done with this Frenchman.

Jackie described their bicycle ride and the way he got her to pose nude for him. Mary couldn't believe Jackie had actually posed for an artist. "What happened to the picture?" Mary wanted to know.

"Funny you should ask. Last night, when I was putting the suitcases away, I found my portrait."

"Let me see it!" Mary said.

Jackie went to the attic and brought the picture down for Mary to see. Mary could hardly wait for her to remove it from the tube. As Jackie unrolled it, Mary couldn't believe her eyes. "My God. It's beautiful. You are beautiful. That is the best portrait I have ever seen!" Mary exclaimed. She studied the drawing for a few minutes and turned to Jackie and said, "What did you think when you saw it for the first time?"

"I was flattered. The feeling that swept over me led to the best sex I ever had. François was an incredible artist and lover. He taught me things I will never forget. We had a relationship through the spring and summer," Jackie said.

As Jackie returned the drawing to its resting place, she told Mary that she was the only person to have seen it except for Barb. "There may be a time that I show it to Jerry, but now is not the right time."

"I can understand how you feel. I don't think I would show a drawing like that of me to John," Mary confessed.

Mary was intent on learning what else took place at the inn. Jackie told her about the couple they met from Philadelphia and that the man had designed the web page for the inn. She told Mary that during the two days they were there they had made love seven times.

"You mean to tell me Jerry was able to perform well each time?" Mary asked.

Jackie assured her the sex was fantastic. "At least I know he still enjoys making love to me. I guess it must be the pressure of work that keeps him from showing me more often," she explained.

After Mary extracted all the details from Jackie, she decided that she and John needed to get away to the inn. Mary asked Jackie for the telephone number so she could see when they could get a reservation. "If I can get John to perform like Jerry, I'll be able to give my vibrator a rest."

"Do you really use that thing?" Jackie inquired.

"Sure. Most times it's the only way I get off. John very seldom takes the time I need to reach climax. It's either the vibrator or I would wind up having an affair with the blond trainer at the spa. He is really a stud. I fantasize doing it with him when I use my vibrator. He has a body that drives me up a wall at times. After a workout with him at the spa, I need a cold shower," Mary explained.

By the time Mary had gotten all the details of Jackie's weekend, it was almost noon. "It's getting late. I must get started on the wash," Jackie said.

"Yes. I'll go home and give the inn a call," responded Mary. "That place is just what the doctor ordered for John and me. Stop over later and we can talk more." Mary got up and went home. Jackie took the wash to the basement and went one step further into her normal routine and one step further from the inn.

It didn't take long for the weeks to pass, and before Jackie knew it, it was late March. Spring was upon her and thoughts of the inn were a fading memory. April was rainy and the cabin fever of the winter continued. Jerry was more consumed than ever by the deals he was trying to put together, and Jackie was becoming frustrated by the lack of attention Jerry paid to her needs. She had gotten away from a scheduled exercise program, and Mary kept after her to get back to a regular program. Jackie decided to take Mary's advice, and they both set up a supervised program three days a week. After a couple of weeks, Jackie was beginning to feel better and took off a few pounds in the right places.

Mary had the hots for the instructor and always talked about what she would like to do with him. Although there was a strict policy of no involvement, Mary tried to flirt with him every once in a while. "Jackie, you should give him a whirl. With a body like yours, I bet he would forget the rules," she said.

"I don't think that's a good idea," Jackie replied. The spa visits did seem to help her focus better, but she was still frustrated with Jerry's lack of attention.

In mid-April, the last parent-teacher conferences were scheduled at school. Jackie got both conferences scheduled on the same morning. Mary watched Lisa and David while Jackie went to school. Lisa's teacher gave a glowing report about Lisa and talked about recommending some enriched work for next year. David's teacher indicated he did very well academically but was a bit of a loner. He seemed to have only one friend, and his teacher thought they should encourage David to join some group or team to help bring him out of his shell.

That night, Jackie talked with Jerry about the teacher conferences. When she told him what David's teacher had had to say, he suggested Pee Wee baseball. David seemed to have some athletic ability and good coordination. Jerry decided to take David to a practice so he could see what it was like. If he showed any interest, they could talk about joining a team.

Jerry also decided to see if John's son, Billie, was going to play ball. He thought if both boys joined the same team, David might be more interested. He seemed to get along with Billie, and they could alternate driving the boys to practice. As it turned out, Billie had decided to join, and Jerry took David to his first practice on Saturday. During practice, David watched as Billie got a couple of hits and saw how much fun he was having. After practice was over, David asked his father if he could join Billy's team. They went over and talked with the coach. At first, the coach indicated they were at their limit, but he would see if they could add one more boy to the roster. As it turned out, one of the boys dropped out, and that provided a spot for David. He began attending practice the following week. Jerry agreed to be an assistant coach, which gave him a good opportunity to observe how well David was progressing both with baseball and with the boys on his team.

Early spring turned into the end of the school year. Jerry had to be away from home on a series of site visits to evaluate several large acquisitions. One was in Hawaii, and Jackie wanted to go along. However, Jerry's schedule and the children's summer plans prevented her from accompanying him.

Jerry was gone a good bit of July and into early August. Jackie was feeling very neglected, and the spa instructor was looking better and better. Jackie would kid Mary about letting her borrow the spa instructor for an afternoon. "You're my best friend, Jackie, but if I could get him for an afternoon, I would keep him all to myself," Mary responded. She did, however, decide to get on the internet and order Jackie a little present. When it arrived, she wrapped it up and took it over to Jackie. Before she gave it to Jackie, Mary made sure the kids weren't around. "Open it," Mary said.

Jackie said, "What is this?" though she suspected by the shape of the package what Mary had gotten her. Yes, it was Jackie's very own vibrator. "What if Jerry finds it? How would I explain it?" she asked.

"Well," answered Mary, "if he finds it, you can say it wasn't as good as he was at the inn, but it was better than nothing."

11

Jackie's Summer

THE SUMMER WAS VERY HOT and dry in Princeton that year. The majority of the July afternoons were in the high nineties, and the first week of August, the temperature was in triple digits. The grass was a light brown color. Jackie had convinced Jerry to hire a lawn service for the first time. The hot summer had destroyed most of the benefits from this care, and Jackie almost wished she hadn't talked Jerry into it.

With Jerry away so much, Jackie's summer was more hectic than normal. She had all her housework and the volunteer work at the nursing home plus all the kids' activities. Mary could see that Jackie was a bit harried and frustrated because of the lack of romance. They discussed how she felt, and Mary convinced Jackie to resume a regular exercise program at the spa. They offered childcare so busy parents could find the time for their workouts. They decided to cut short their morning coffee and go to the spa at ten o'clock Mondays, Wednesdays, and Fridays. Mary hoped this would help take Jackie's mind off Jerry's lack of attention and help keep her body in shape.

It was Wednesday, and Jackie's turn to host the morning coffee. Mary was a bit early and appeared in the kitchen before eight o'clock. She took one look at Jackie and said, "You look strung out! Is there anything I can do to help?"

"No. In a little over a week Jerry gets home, and then I'll be OK."

"You need some help before that," Mary insisted.

Mary knew Jackie wouldn't ask, so she decided to invite Lisa and David over on Friday night for a sleepover. This would give Jackie a chance to unwind. "The kids can come over about five, and we'll get pizza and take them miniature golfing. After that, we have the video *Mouse Hunt* that the kids all love."

"You don't have to go to all that trouble," Jackie said.

"It's no trouble. We love to have the kids over, and Billie will have fun as well."

Jackie finally agreed and thanked Mary.

The girls finished their coffee, and Mary went home to give Billie breakfast. Jackie did the same for Lisa and David. She called the kids to come down for breakfast, and in a few minutes Lisa and David appeared at the table. Lisa wanted some Cocoa Puffs, and David, French toast. Jackie decided on an English muffin and some juice. After they finished their breakfast, Jackie told them to hurry and get dressed in order to get to the spa by ten. As she cleaned up the breakfast dishes, she began to plan her Friday evening alone. Her thoughts turned to the vibrator that Mary had given her. She had never had it out of the box and wondered what it would be like. Before long, the kids appeared, and it was off to the spa.

Hump day passed slowly, but it finally came to an end with Jackie tucking the kids into bed. The phone rang. It was Jerry calling before he went to a late-night dinner meeting. Jackie told him of her day and that Mary and John were going to have the kids over Friday night. Jerry thought that was a good idea and would give Jackie some badly needed time alone. "What will you do on Friday night?" he asked.

"I plan to take a long bath and will probably read my new book in bed." She didn't mention her plan to get acquainted with her vibrator. After all, she had never told Jerry about it.

"Do you miss me?" Jerry asked.

"You know I do, you silly pill. You better get yourself home next Friday, and don't be tired. I will require some attention from you," Jackie said.

"What did you have in mind?" Jerry inquired.

"You know exactly what I'll need. I plan to have the kids at my parents Saturday evening by the time you get home. Don't be late," Jackie insisted. They said goodbye, and Jackie decided to watch some TV before going to bed.

Thursday passed quickly, and by Friday, Jackie's thoughts turned more and more to her evening alone. The girls got to the spa, and Jackie thought how great the trainer Paul looked. Mary was always the one who talked about him, and upon closer examination, Jackie could see he was quite a hunk. After their workout, they took the kids for lunch and went home. The kids decided to play together at Mary's, and Jackie went home. She decided to take a look at the vibrator and see what size batteries it took. She opened it up and saw it took D batteries.

Finding that all she had were AA and C, she called Mary to tell her that she had to run to the store and pick up some D batteries.

"And what do you need with D batteries?" Mary jokingly asked.

"Never you mind," Jackie responded.

"You can borrow some of mine. I have the rechargeable type. Come over and I'll give you what you need," Mary said.

Jackie got the batteries and returned home.

It was soon five o'clock, and Jackie finished getting the kids' pajamas and toothbrushes ready. Lisa and David had returned home and were playing their video games in the recreation room. "It's time to go over to Mary's," Jackie said. The kids turned off the game and ran for the door. Jackie followed them with their clothing and gave them a hug. "You have fun and listen to Mary. I will see you tomorrow morning. I love you." By this time, it was going on six, and she decided on takeout Chinese for her dinner.

Jackie got out the menu from their favorite Chinese restaurant and decided what to order. She called in her order, and they told her she could pick it up in a few minutes. She grabbed her keys and purse and drove to the restaurant. When she arrived home, she got out a bottle of wine and proceeded to spread her dinner out on the family room floor. She popped in a travel video and ate a relaxing dinner. Jackie had several glasses of wine, which had a tendency to mellow her a bit. About the time she finished her dinner, Jerry called to see how she was. He told her he was about to go out for a working dinner and that he had a site visit on Saturday.

After Jerry's call, Jackie decided to clean up the dinner dishes and get ready for her bath. She turned the lights off on the first floor and went upstairs. She got out the vibrator and installed the batteries Mary had given her. She turned the dial and the vibrator began to hum. As she turned the control to the right, the vibrator shook faster and faster. Jackie turned it off and laid it on the bed. She went into the bathroom and started running the water. She wanted it hot and added a liberal amount of the new bath salts she'd purchased. She went to the linen closet and got out an oversized towel to wrap herself in when she got out of the tub.

When the tub was filled, Jackie took off her clothing and stepped into the water. It felt so good. She leaned her head back and rested it on an inflatable headrest. For over an hour, Jackie allowed the water to caress her body. She almost fell asleep several times, and as the water began to cool off, she decided to get out and dry off. After she was dry, she let the water out of the tub and went into the bedroom.

Even though she knew she was alone in the house, Jackie closed the door to make sure no one saw her. She took off the towel and lay on the bed. She turned the vibrator on and began to touch it to her breasts. It felt tingly but good. Slowly she moved the oscillating tool between her breasts and toward her tummy. She lingered there a few seconds as if she was teasing herself before she moved ever closer to the intended spot. All the time she was using it she was fantasizing that Paul the trainer was using the toy on her. She closed her eyes to imagine his face as he moved it toward her waiting love spot.

She finally got the courage to place the tip of it on her womanhood. She rubbed it all over and slowly increased the speed. It wasn't long before Jackie was fully engrossed with her new toy. She let out a scream as it did the job, and it was then that Jackie knew why Mary used one. She lay on the bed for some time after she had finished and finally got up to wash her new toy and put it away. She put on her nightgown and got under the covers. Mary was right: it wasn't as good as Jerry, but it wasn't bad. *In fact*, she thought, *I'm going to use it again.*

12

Jackie Revisits Friday Night at the Inn

JACKIE SLEPT STRAIGHT THROUGH THE NIGHT. Generally she woke up at least once, but her Friday activities helped her sleep through the night. At eight thirty she was awakened by David, who called her from Mary's. While the kids ate breakfast at Mary's, Jackie decided to have some Rice Krispies and coffee before Lisa and David came home. Soon after she finished, David and Lisa tumbled in the back door.

"Hi, Mom. Guess who won the miniature golf last night," David said.

That was easy: David would not have asked unless he had won. Jackie said, "Let me see . . . Lisa won."

"Mom. Guess again," said David.

Jackie was in a teasing mood and said, "Billie."

"No! I won," David announced.

David and Lisa had been invited to their cousin's birthday party that afternoon. Jackie told the kids to get their cousin's presents so they could wrap them. After they finished, the kids went out to play, and about eleven, Jackie gave them some fruit to hold them until the party.

After they finished, they got dressed in clean clothing, and Jackie drove them to her sisters.

Jackie had to hurry home because she was expecting the grocery store to deliver her order. She decided to make a light dinner, so she took some hot dogs and potatoes from the refrigerator. She put the hot dogs on the stove to cook, and while they were boiling, she cut up some hard-boiled eggs, potatoes, celery, onions, and olives to mix into a salad.

It was about two when she heard a knock at the back door. It was the delivery boy with her order. She opened the door and said, "You're new. I don't remember you delivering my order before."

"You're right. My name is Chris, and I just started at the grocery store about two weeks ago."

"Do you live around here, Chris?" Jackie asked.

"Yes. I'm a student at Princeton. I needed some extra money, and this job seemed to fit into my schedule," he replied.

Jackie looked him over and thought, *What a stud. He's better looking than the trainer at the spa.* She had the feeling she had seen him before. "Are you sure we've never met?" Jackie asked.

"I don't think so."

Jackie playfully said, "Call me Jackie." She asked him to place the bags on the counter and the kitchen table. "I had a large order this week," she remarked. "Could you give me a hand putting it away?"

"Sure. I'll hand it to you and you can place it on the shelves."

As Chris was handing the groceries to Jackie, a bag of jelly beans slipped out of his hand and split open on the floor. Chris knelt down to pick up the candy, and Jackie moved closer to him, so that he was staring directly into her lap. Jackie was feeling playful, and Chris was aware of what she was doing. Jackie wondered if he would react to her teasing him.

Chris decided to see how far he could go and placed his hand on Jackie's leg. He moved it up just under the edge of her shorts. Jackie was startled, and for a few seconds she didn't react. Chris took that to be a green light and moved his hand under her shorts until he touched her most private part. At that moment Jackie remembered her dream at the inn. She jumped away from Chris and said, "What do you think you're doing? Get out of here before I call your boss." Chris was both startled and afraid. He quickly got up and drove off in his delivery truck without saying a word.

Jackie was so unnerved by this she locked the doors and went up to her bedroom. She didn't know if she was more disturbed by what Chris had done or by the fact that it was an exact replay of the dream she'd had six months earlier. When she tried to recall the name and face of the delivery boy in her dream, she knew it was Chris. In addition, the name of the grocery store manager was Dan Jones and he was a friend of Jerry's. How could this be true? It wasn't possible to dream what would happen in the future. This was the most bizarre event that Jackie had ever experienced.

She thought, *What if I hadn't stopped him? Would I have gotten myself into the situation in my dream?* Jackie was so disturbed she didn't finish putting the rest of the groceries away. About four o'clock the phone rang. It was David. He wanted to know if they could have dinner at his aunt's.

"Put your aunt on the phone," Jackie said. "Brenda, are you sure you want the kids for dinner?"

"Yes. We'll bring them home after seven. They're having a good time, and I would like them to stay. Why don't you come over too."

Jackie said, "No, thanks. I appreciate you feeding the kids. See you later."

Jackie was glad Brenda had asked the kids for dinner. She didn't feel much like making dinner. She had some fruit and milk for her dinner. She wasn't very hungry. It was seven thirty when Brenda knocked at the door with the kids.

"Come in and stay awhile," Jackie said.

"No, thanks. I need to get home and clean up from the party."

Lisa and David were anxious to tell their mother about the games they'd played at the party. Jackie pretended to listen to them, but her mind was on the events of that afternoon. She got the kids off to bed and decided to rest on the sofa in the family room for a while. She pondered the afternoon, and about ten o'clock she decided to get into bed.

There was nothing special on the agenda for Sunday. She took the kids to Sunday school, and they stopped for brunch before returning home. Jackie couldn't relax or get the incident off her mind. She wanted to call the store manager, but she knew that would get the delivery boy in a great deal of trouble. Jerry would also find out what took place, and she knew he would be angry and want to go to the police. She wondered if she could have sent Chris the wrong signal. She knew boys, especially at that age, had raging hormones. She also knew that she didn't stop Chris when he put his hand on her leg or object until his fingers touched her female parts. In fact, Jackie wasn't sure what would have happened had it not been for her dream. Could she have ended up on the kitchen table with this young man?

Jackie desperately wanted to discuss it with Mary. She knew there was no one else she would trust in talking about either her dream or the incident with Chris. Jackie decided to call Mary Sunday night to make sure they were getting together the next morning. "I have something very important to discuss with you," she said.

"Do you want me to come over now?" Mary asked.

"No. I don't want to alarm John. It can wait until tomorrow morning," Jackie said.

The next morning, Mary knocked at the door and walked into the kitchen. "Hi. What's on your mind? You sounded so concerned last night."

Jackie said, "Please sit down and have some coffee. You'll need several cups until I finish." She proceeded to tell Mary all about her dream at the inn.

At first, Mary didn't understand the significance of her dream until she told her what took place with Chris Saturday afternoon. At first, Mary tried to dismiss it as a bazaar coincidence. However, as Jackie went into more and more detail, Mary realized this was more than that. Much more.

Mary wanted to know if Jackie planned to report Chris to the police or the store manager. Jackie told her that at first she meant to, but she didn't want Jerry to find out. She also admitted that she might have encouraged Chris a little. After talking it over with Mary, she decided to say nothing. She wouldn't have groceries delivered and would shop at a different store in the future. So long as Chris didn't attempt to have any further contact with her, Jackie decided to put the incident behind her.

Even though Jackie was somewhat successful in putting the incident with Chris out of her mind, she couldn't explain how the dream had occurred in the first place. After all, it isn't possible to know the future. However, in reality, that was just what happened to Jackie that February night.

13

Revelation

Jerry arrived home the following Friday, and Jackie ran to greet him as he got out of the car. She hugged and kissed him as they walked to the back door. "It looks like I was missed," Jerry said. He had no idea how glad Jackie was that he was home. "Are the kids at your parents?" he asked.

"Yes, I dropped them off about four o'clock," Jackie answered.

Jackie told Jerry everything that had been going on except the most important thing—Chris and her dream. Jerry sensed Jackie was disturbed about something, but when he questioned her, she just shrugged it off. They decided to go out for dinner and wound up at the local pizza place. By the time they were done eating, Jackie had some other activity on her mind.

As soon as they arrived home, Jackie took a shower and got into bed buck naked. She pulled the sheet up to her neck and called down to Jerry to come tuck her in.

Jerry came into the bedroom and shut the door. He walked to the edge of the bed and pulled the sheet down. "It looks like you're ready for business!"

"Come into my bed and I'll show you," Jackie responded. This was the first time she could put the incident with Chris out of her mind. They made love two times that night.

Saturday morning found Jackie at ease and happy to greet the day. She lay next to Jerry and knew their relationship was strong. She felt secure, loved, and happy to be with him. She craved the closeness that most women want, and she needed the physical side of the relationship.

The hot summer began to give way as the school year approached. Jackie and Jerry had decided last spring that it was time for Jackie to return to teaching. She had stopped when David was born, but now Lisa and David were in school and Jackie wanted to resume her career. It wasn't that they needed the money, but Jackie needed to be fulfilled. Jerry recognized this and suggested they hire a cleaning woman to come in on Saturdays to give a hand with the housework.

As it turned out, Jackie was rehired as a first-grade teacher. When she had left teaching, she was an art teacher, but there were no vacancies in art. The school district had started a policy where the elementary teachers followed the pupils for three years. Thus, Jackie would have the same class for first, second, and third grades. She would then begin with a new class in year four in the first grade. This was intended to be a better way for the teachers to help the kids achieve their full potential.

It seemed that Jackie's return to teaching, and some added attention from Jerry, helped her to forget the problem with Chris. For the first time since the kids were born, Jackie seemed content and truly happy. Beth came every Saturday about nine o'clock to clean the house and do the wash. She got along well with the kids, and they had a game to see which one did the best job of keeping their room straight. Beth would bring little treats. The first prize was always better than the one for the runner-up, so there was competition to be the best.

The fall and winter passed quickly. Maybe it was all the kids' activities, or maybe it was Jackie working. Whatever the reason, it flew by. One of the things Jackie and Mary had wanted to do was to get a reservation at the inn for both of them. By the time they called, there were no vacancies on the weekends that suited them. They pledged that they would make reservations for next winter just as soon as Jackie had the calendar for the school year.

Before long, it was spring. The snow in Princeton lingered, and it took the April rains to wash away the last reminder of winter. One morning in May, Jerry folded his paper so he could read it without disturbing the person next to him. It was a familiar sight to a commuter, and one that Jerry had repeated many times.

As he began reading the financial section, he spotted an article about Alpha Investments. This was a company Dave, his broker, had tried to get Jerry to buy six months earlier. The article described the success of this IPO. Since November, its stock had increased sevenfold. Jerry knew he had screwed up, but he wasn't too disappointed because he knew there would be other opportunities.

Jerry got into the office about 8:45 and had just poured a cup of coffee when the phone rang. It was Dave.

"Did you read the article about Alpha in this morning's paper?" he asked.

"Yes. I know you told me it was a great buy. I made a mistake," Jerry acknowledged.

Dave and Jerry had been close since their days at Penn, and they kidded each other all the time.

"All is forgiven. I have a great one for you today. The firm is called Surgical Ventures. They have developed—"

"A glue that is used in place of stitches," said Jerry.

"How in the devil did you know that?" Dave asked.

"You mean that *is* what they developed?" Jerry asked.

"That's right. Did you get another broker?" Dave asked.

"You know I only trust you, Dave," Jerry said. He had remembered his dream when Dave told him the name of the company and had just blurted out the part about the glue. Jerry asked Dave to fax the prospectus. "How many shares will be available?"

Dave responded, "I think I can get you five thousand at ten dollars per share. You'll have to make up your mind fast so I can reserve the shares."

After Dave hung up, Jerry began to recall his dream. *My God*, he thought, *I also dreamt about the Alpha article.* There were five thousand shares at ten dollars per share in his dream as well. What was happening? As soon as Dave's fax arrived, Jerry asked his secretary, Tiffany, to hold his calls unless it was Dave or Jackie. Reading over the material, it was as if he were replaying his February dream. Jerry took out a pad and tried to remember how the deal had ended in his dream. He was a bit confused because he'd dreamt about three separate incidents that night, and he was having a little trouble sorting them out. He finally remembered he'd purchased the five thousand shares for ten dollars each and sold them four months later at eighty dollars per share, making a tidy $350K on the deal.

Jerry decided to jot down his recollection of the other two dreams as well. The Optiscan was intended to identify a person by scanning the iris of the eye. As he recalled, it had two cameras: the first located the eye with one camera, and the other zoomed in to scan the iris. It only took several seconds and worked through glasses and contacts. He remembered buying twelve thousand shares at fifteen dollars per share and that he was a little uneasy about investing that much money. However, Dave pointed out how well he'd done with Surgical Ventures, which convinced Jerry to buy all twelve thousand shares. He also remembered it had been December when he bought the shares and March when he sold them for eighty-eight dollars per share. That deal made him 875 grand.

Jerry's thoughts then turned to his final dream, which was the market crash. This was the one from which he'd woken up in a cold sweat. It had started on Thursday, April 14. He was on the links with his boss when they both got calls on their cell phones. The Dow dropped twenty-five hundred points on the fourteenth and another three thousand on the fifteenth. The losses were twenty to one, and the crash was the result of a problem in the Middle East and a cutoff of oil shipments. He remembered how he'd lost most of his holdings and been sold out because he couldn't meet the margin call. He also recalled that the market had closed at 2:00 p.m. on the fifteenth because of the near panic on Wall Street.

Jerry returned to reading the material Dave had faxed to him. He decided to sleep on the purchase and put the fax in his briefcase. Throughout the day, Jerry couldn't help but think how bizarre this whole thing was. People didn't dream about reality before it happened. How could the events of the day have been so close to that dream? He did recall how real the dream had seemed at the time.

Jerry didn't generally discuss his investments with Jackie until after the results were complete. He hadn't told her of his dream nor about the stock market crash. He didn't want to upset her, and he decided not to say anything about the events of the day or his February dream at the inn.

After the market closed, Dave called again. He was disturbed that Jerry knew about his recommendation. "Why won't you come clean with me as to where you learned about the glue? That was closely held. I only found out last night. You were the first client I called."

"It just popped into my head, Dave."

"Well, if you keep that up, I want you to go to the track with me," Dave said.

Jerry told him he would let him know Monday morning about the IPO. Dave said that was fine, and they hung up.

14

More Revelations

Jerry was preoccupied for the next several days. Jackie thought it was his concern about some of the acquisitions at work. She had no idea their weekend at the inn was behind Jerry's thoughts. He couldn't help but wonder if this was all just a strange, unexplained incident, or if it was an opportunity to pierce the veil that guarded the future. Should he act on the dream, or should he make his investment decision based on the facts Dave provided? In the final analysis, Jerry made his decision to purchase the five thousand shares of Surgical Ventures because it looked like a good investment.

On Monday morning, Jerry called Dave about 8:45 and instructed him to purchase the stock. On Wednesday, Dave called to confirm that Jerry was the owner of five thousand shares of Surgical Ventures at the expected ten dollars per share. Jerry told Dave he would transfer the funds for payment after lunch.

From the outset, Surgical Ventures skyrocketed, and within three months, it was selling at fifty dollars per share. Two weeks later a rumor was on the street that a large pharmaceutical company was trying to buy Surgical Ventures. When Jerry learned of this, his thoughts immediately went back to his dream. In Jerry's dream, that was exactly what Dave said might take place. According to his dream, by the time four months had passed from Jerry's purchase the stock would be selling at eighty dollars and he would sell it.

In another two weeks, just four months from its initial offering, the pharmaceutical company announced that an agreement had been finalized for it to acquire Surgical Ventures. The price shot up to eighty dollars. Dave called to advise Jerry to sell and take his profit. Dave admitted it might have a further run-up, but he thought it was good to take his profit. Jerry agreed and instructed Dave to sell all five thousand shares.

"Call me back as soon as it's sold."

"Will do."

That afternoon Dave called to inform Jerry he was 350 grand richer. Jerry thanked Dave and told him, "I owe you a first-class dinner."

Jerry was anxious to tell Jackie of their good fortune, but still wasn't convinced he should tell her about his dreams. He didn't know what to think of it himself. In the end, he decided to omit that part of the story. He would tell Jackie about the dreams if the Optiscan IPO developed as it did in his second dream.

Jackie was very excited by the news, and she knew it moved them one step closer to financial independence. She was proud of her husband and his ability to provide for their family.

The summer spilled into late fall with winter not far behind. It seemed like a flash and it was December. Jerry was in his office looking out of his thirtieth-floor window when the first snow began to fall in New York. The sight of the snow caused a flashback to his dream again. He recalled that it was the day of the first snow that Dave called about Optiscan. No sooner had this thought crept into Jerry's head than the phone rang. It was Dave.

"Jerry, I have the best IPO for you yet," Dave said.

"You always tell me that, Dave."

"No, I mean it. This company has developed an identification system that scans the iris of the eye. The company's name is Optiscan."

Jerry went into shock. He said nothing and let Dave tell him the all too familiar story of how it worked and the financial particulars. When Dave was finished, he wanted to know what Jerry thought. Jerry didn't want him to know how disturbing this revelation was and told Dave to fax him the material.

"OK," Dave said. "However, you must act quickly. This one is hot. I think I can get you ten thousand shares at fifteen dollars per share."

Dave hung up, and Jerry sat back in his chair in a daze.

After a few minutes, Jerry called Tiffany to come into his office. "I will be receiving a fax from Dave. Please bring it in as soon as it arrives. I also want you to hold my calls unless it's Dave or my wife, and check my calendar for the balance of the day. I may want to leave the office early."

Tiffany thought this was odd, for Jerry never left the office early unless he had an appointment. As it turned out, Jerry was clear for the balance of the day, though he did have a ten o'clock meeting the next morning with his boss.

Jerry took out the notes he had made about his dreams after his first dream came true, and waited for Tiffany to bring him Dave's fax. It arrived in about fifteen minutes, and he began comparing the material Dave had sent with his notes of his second dream. It was as if some unseen director were calling the shots. The prospectus was exactly like Jerry's notes of his dream. After comparing the data, he put everything in his briefcase and told Tiffany he would be leaving. He had to check the train schedule because he didn't know it that early in the day. He decided to put his rubbers over his shoes, for there was over an inch of snow on the ground. Jerry walked as if in a daze to the train station. The events of the day were almost beyond comprehension. He arrived a few minutes before the train pulled into the station.

He was one of the first passengers to board and could sit wherever he liked. He selected a window seat and got comfortable as the train began pulling away from the station. Almost immediately, Jerry's mind returned to that fateful weekend last February. He recalled the expression he and Jackie saw on the registration clerk's face when he handed them the key to room D. It was as if the clerk was trying to convey something more than just handing them a key. Neither had commented about it at the time, but they did mention it to each other Friday night over drinks.

Jerry also thought back to the message on the bottom of his statement when he checked out of the inn—". . . and hope all your dreams come true." The odd thing about this was that the statement on Frank's receipt was not the same. It said nothing about dreams. Jerry remembered he hadn't understood why there would be different messages on the receipts. At the time, neither of these quirks warranted a second thought. In fact, both of them together didn't register. However, now that Jerry's second dream was coming true, they seemed to be part of something far greater than anyone could imagine.

The clatter of the train wheels lulled Jerry into a state that might be called day dreaming. It was as if reality and fantasy had become intertwined, and it was hard to tell one from the other. He wasn't sure how to make Jackie understand or believe what he was about to tell her without sounding like a nutcase. After all, Jerry was a key executive in a well-respected firm on Wall Street. How could he tell his wife that his dreams saw into the future?

Jerry took out his notes recalling the dreams. He compared them with the information Dave had faxed him on Optiscan. There was no denying it: the information was identical. Jerry had the option of doing the same thing he had done with Surgical Ventures and evaluate it based on the financial data Dave had provided. He could then make a judgment with little reliance on the predictions of his dreams. But Jerry was having a dilemma with the third dream. It, unlike the other two, gave insight into a market crash and a financial disaster. At the same time, he knew that the opportunity to make money in a down market was generally greater than in an up market. However, he also considered another aspect of the crash. It would have an adverse impact on his friends who were in the market big time, as well as on their parents so far as their retirement investments were concerned.

The ride home was all too short to prepare him for the task of confronting his wife with this news. Jerry quickly got off the train and into his car. He thought of getting some coffee at the diner before going home but decided to skip it and go home to Jackie. After all, she was his wife and would accept what he had to tell her. The sooner she knew the better.

Jerry pulled into the drive just as Jackie got home from school. "What are you doing home at this hour?" she questioned.

"We need to talk."

Jackie could tell from Jerry's tone that something important was up.

He began to tell her of his dreams that February night at the inn. He told her about the Alpha deal he missed and how the dream described the Surgical Ventures deal that had provided over a third of a million dollars in profit for them. He reminded her of how she had awakened him from his sleep when she wanted to have sex in the middle of the night.

Jerry then told her of the other two dreams he'd had that night. He explained that the first of these two dreams described an IPO for a company that developed an identification system that scanned the eye. He showed her the material Dave had sent on Optiscan. "This is exactly like my dream," he said. He then went into the most disturbing aspect—the dream about the market crash in April. He briefly explained how in two days most of their investments were destroyed by a major political and economic disaster in the Middle East. He told Jackie of the fifty-five-hundred-point drop in the Dow in just two days.

Jackie examined the notes Jerry had made about his dreams. She was very shook up by what he had told her. She showed a stronger reaction than he had expected, but Jerry didn't know about her dream and the incident with Chris. Jackie was dumbfounded. No way could this be happening. Yet she, too, felt that her dream was very real, but she never thought anything like this could happen. Jackie didn't want to tell

Jerry about Chris, but, in the end, she knew he must know. It looked as though both of them had been given a glimpse into their futures.

Jackie said to Jerry, "Now it's my turn to blow your mind."

She began by telling him about her dream on Friday night at the inn. Jerry was angry at first to think she would dream of being unfaithful. Jackie assured him it was just a dream and that she would never do something like that.

After Jerry calmed down a bit, he turned to Jackie and said, "What does that have to do with what I told you? How will this blow my mind?" he asked.

She proceeded to tell him about her grocery delivery last Saturday and how the new delivery boy, Chris, put his hand on her private parts. Jerry exploded.

"What the hell did you do?"

Jackie answered, "I told him to get out and that I was thinking of calling his boss." She explained that she was going to call Mr. Jones, but she didn't want to upset Jerry. "You have enough with work, and I decided that if there were no further contact with Chris, I wouldn't say anything." Jackie further explained that, as she thought back over her dream, everything up to the point where Chris touched her was just like her dream. Jackie told Jerry how much this had bothered her all week and that she was torn between telling him and not wanting to upset him.

"Did you tell anyone else about what happened?" Jerry wanted to know.

"Yes," Jackie admitted. "I told Mary both about the dream and about Chris. She was as confused as I was."

"This does cast my dreams in a new light," Jerry said. "It seems that somehow we both dreamt about our future. In your case, you stopped Chris before the remainder of the events took place. However, who knows, if you hadn't stopped him, would all the events in your dream have become reality? The question now is, Will the unfulfilled portions of my dreams come true?"

The answer to that question had great significance to Jackie and Jerry as well as their friends and family. The market crash portrayed in his last dream would hurt not only Jackie and Jerry but also Dave, John, and Mary. It would also hurt their parents, who had much of their retirement savings in the market. If they believed this was a hint of things to come, what should they do with this knowledge? The answer to this question would prove to be a defining moment in the lives of their family and friends.

After the shock of the dreams wore off a bit, Jerry began to look at the situation using the logical process he used on decisions at work. After all, here was a man who evaluated major issues every day and handled them in a businesslike way. When Jerry considered a potential acquisition, he had the factual information on which to base his decision. As far as the purchase of the IPOs, Jerry had the facts that Dave had provided, and the predictions from his dream weren't essential for him to buy or not buy Optiscan. The question of how Jerry could have known the facts before they became facts was unanswered. The more perplexing issue was his last dream about the market crash. This matter had no facts that could be used to decide if this would take place. No one in the world had any indication that a situation would develop in the Middle East that would cause the market to crash fifteen months from now.

Jackie had almost forgotten about the kids, who had been playing in their rooms. "Jerry, we must get dinner for the kids," she reminded him. "We can continue our discussion after the kids have eaten."

Jerry got up and asked the kids what they wanted for dinner. As usual, Lisa and David wanted pizza. It was already dark and very cold on this December night. Jerry decided to have the pizza delivered so they didn't have to go out in the cold. He called in their order, and the pizza parlor said it would take about thirty minutes. They set up to eat in the family room by the fireplace and waited for their pizza. It arrived about five thirty, and it wasn't long before they had finished their dinner.

The kids wanted to watch a video, which gave Jackie and Jerry a chance to continue their important discussion.

They started the video for Lisa and David and went back to the kitchen. Jackie asked, "Do you want some coffee?"

"That sounds good. Make it a big pot," Jerry responded. He started by pointing out that there was no certainty that the rest of his dreams would come true. After all, Jackie's dream didn't totally come true. Jackie pointed out that was because she chose not to follow the dream, knowing what the consequences would be. There was no telling what would have happened if she had allowed Chris to finish what he started. There was no question in Jackie's mind that he would have had sex with her if she hadn't stopped him.

Jerry couldn't deny what Jackie was saying. "Well, let's just say the remainder of my dreams will come true. If we invest in Optiscan, we will make a lot of money. If we don't, the opportunity will pass us by and in three months we'll be kicking ourselves. However, the issue with the last dream and the market crash is a much more serious problem. This could wipe us out, along with family and friends."

Should Jerry treat his last dream as the prediction it seemed to be and try to convince others of the impending disaster? Truly, they were faced with decisions that would prove to be defining moments in their lives and in the lives of anyone who believed Jerry's dreams.

The kid's video was over, and it was time for them to go to bed. Jackie went up to supervise their baths and preparations for bed. Lisa got her bath first and wanted her daddy to read a story. She called to him, and Jerry walked up the stairs to her bedroom. Lisa selected *The Little Engine That Could*. David finished his bath about the time Jerry had finished reading Lisa her story, and the kids were tucked in for the night.

Jackie and Jerry returned to the kitchen for another cup of coffee and continued their discussion. Their conversation returned to their February weekend, and they both tried to recall any details that would help shed light on this dilemma. Jerry reviewed the expression on the face of the clerk when they received the key to room D. Jerry also talked about the different messages on the receipts. At that point, Jackie got up and went over to the desk in the kitchen. She pulled out the receipt with the message about their dreams. "Sure enough, the message on the receipt says, 'We hope all your dreams come true,'" Jackie said.

Jerry said, "It's almost like there was something about the room. I wonder if anyone else who stayed in room D had similar dreams."

"Wouldn't that be something," Jackie responded.

"That gives me an idea," Jerry said. "Let's see if we can track down others who stayed at the inn in room D."

Jackie agreed and said she would begin with the staff at the inn to see if they would cooperate. She would also see if she could locate other guests from the Inn of Destiny online.

Jerry returned the discussion to the IPO and Optiscan. Jackie agreed with his point that the choice to buy this stock should be made the same way Jerry made the decision to purchase other investments. After all, he had a great track record, and they had a very successful investment program. Jerry decided that the facts provided by Dave showed a high probability of success, and he would instruct him to purchase the shares in Optiscan for their account. By this time, it was past midnight and they decided to call it a night. Even though it was a bit later than they normally went to bed, Jackie wanted them to enjoy each other before ending this eventful day.

15

Search for Answers

Jackie woke up just before the faithful alarm clock announced it was time to begin another day. Her thoughts returned to their dreams and the discussion with Jerry the previous night.

Jerry was still asleep when the alarm rang. He rolled out of bed and into the shower. He could feel the rising tension of both his dreams and the large acquisitions he had to decide on within a week or two. In fact, that was the subject of his meeting that morning with his boss. Since he wanted to talk with Dave about his decision to purchase the Optiscan stock before his ten o'clock meeting, he had to make sure he got the 7:20. Like Jackie, Jerry's thoughts were fully taken up with what this all would mean. He was glad he had settled the matter of the IPO, but he knew if the deal unfolded the way it had in his dream, it would increase the tension on what the third dream meant to him.

He got dressed and went down for a hurried breakfast. "I'll call Dave as soon as I get into the office and tell him to purchase the Optiscan for us," Jerry said.

"Fine. I'm glad we talked it over last night. I'll see if I can locate other couples that may have stayed in our room at the inn," Jackie replied.

Jerry finished his coffee and kissed the kids and Jackie goodbye. He made sure to put the information about Optiscan and the material for the meeting in his briefcase. He arrived at the station about 7:10 a.m., and the train pulled in on time. As he settled into the seat, he desperately tried to concentrate on the upcoming meeting with his boss. However, thoughts about the market crash and the potential consequences occupied his mind.

When he arrived at the office, he called Dave, who was expecting his call.

"Well, what do you think of Optiscan?" Dave asked.

"It looks as good as you said," Jerry answered.

Dave said, "I think I may be able to get you an additional two thousand shares, for a total of twelve thousand, at fifteen dollars per share. I think you should take them all given the outstanding potential of the company." This was an exact replay of the February dream, and Jerry told Dave to go ahead and buy all twelve thousand shares for his account.

"Let me know the exact amount, and I will transfer the funds from the bank to you," Jerry said.

"I think you've made another great decision. I'll call you as soon as I have confirmation of the purchase. This deal should make you a millionaire," Dave responded.

After they hung up, Jerry put the material on Optiscan back in his briefcase and began getting ready for his ten o'clock meeting.

As it turned out, the proposed acquisition was a large shopping center in Florida. The current owner was a member of the Saudi royal family. *How ironic*, Jerry thought. He was about to enter into a business agreement with someone who would be a part of the crisis that would cause the stock market to crash in about sixteen months. As he reviewed the proposal, Jerry couldn't help but wonder if they should go ahead with it. Because it appeared to be a good deal for Jerry's firm, he couldn't figure out how to tell his boss they shouldn't buy it. How could he tell his boss that they shouldn't buy it because he'd dreamed that the stock market was going to crash?

Jerry picked up the charts and financial statements and headed for Mr. Hagman's office. Barry Hagman was a very successful man who made sure others knew of his achievements. Everything he did was first class. His office was no exception. As you approached the area surrounding his office, the first thing that greeted you were two junior secretaries. For most people that was as far as they got. You had to either be very important or have been summoned by Mr. Hagman to reach the second plateau: Miss Finch, his private secretary. In the waiting area was a series of tables and leather furniture as well as an eighteenth-century grandfather clock. Just by the way the outer office was appointed, you knew you were in the middle of success. Jerry was the number-two man in the firm, and he went directly to Miss Finch's desk.

"Hello, how are you this morning, Miss Finch?" Jerry asked.

"Fine, Mr. French. Would you like some coffee?"

"No, thanks. I'm trying to cut down a bit. However, I would like a glass of orange juice," Jerry said. Miss Finch picked up the intercom and asked the steward in charge of the executive dining room to bring a glass of juice.

Almost immediately, the steward appeared with a tall glass of orange juice and a linen napkin. Jerry thanked him, and just as the grandfather clock struck ten, Mr. Hagman opened his door.

"Come in, Jerry." He turned to Miss Finch and asked her to have the steward bring fresh coffee, juice, sweet rolls, and fruit into his office.

Jerry sat at the large conference table located in such a way that one could look out the windows onto Wall Street far below. All of this was in keeping with the success that the firm had enjoyed.

Everything in Mr. Hagman's office was the best, from his huge desk to the exquisite oriental rugs on the floor. To the left of the office was a door that led into the executive dining room, and there was a huge bathroom, complete with a sauna, on the right side of the office. On the other side of the bathroom was a large bedroom with a projection TV and sound system.

Barry Hagman sat across from Jerry, and they were about to get started when the steward brought in the refreshments Mr. Hagman had ordered. "Jerry, what would you like for lunch?" he asked.

"Bring me a chicken Caesar salad and assorted cheeses," Jerry answered.

"Bring me a steak," Mr. Hagman said, and the steward left the room and closed the door.

The discussion lasted until lunch, and they retired to the dining room about noon. Mr. Hagman had asked the CFO, Ben Decker, to join them to discuss the financing options for the proposed acquisitions.

By the time Jerry and Mr. Hagman arrived in the dining room, Ben was waiting for them. He had ordered a salmon steak for his lunch and was enjoying a Scotch before his meal.

"Hi, Ben, glad to see you," Mr. Hagman said. Jerry went over and shook Ben's hand, and the three men sat down at the table. Mr. Hagman ordered a glass of wine, and Jerry had a whiskey. The steward arrived in a few minutes and served the noon meal. As usual, it was outstanding, for the steward's only responsibility was to ensure that Mr. Hagman and his guests had only the very best meals possible each day. On occasion, the steward would also prepare dinner if there was a late meeting scheduled.

The men didn't talk business during lunch, as Mr. Hagman believed this was a time to relax from the morning business and get ready for the remainder of the day. After lunch was finished, they returned to Mr. Hagman's office and began reviewing the financing options for each acquisition. Ben favored using long-term debt because the interest rates were so low. He didn't see the rate dropping much further, so there was no reason to start with short-term funding and later convert to permanent options.

They reviewed the purchase ranges for each property to ensure they were all in agreement with the parameters that Jerry would use to negotiate the final purchase of each property. They had set a tentative range when they evaluated the properties earlier. At this point, they were still interested in all the acquisitions on their list, and it was just a matter of fine-tuning the ranges. In reality, Jerry had the authority to exceed the ranges, but they were thought of as targets to help in the negotiations. The only property that they reviewed in detail was the shopping center in Florida. That was the largest dollar project and the most complex to analyze.

Ben kept notes on their discussion and told them he would have the summary ready for them early the next morning. Both Jerry and Mr. Hagman wanted to review it over the weekend, as the negotiations on the first few properties were to begin within ten days. Jerry hoped to have all the purchases finalized by the early part of January, with settlement in February.

They completed their meeting about four o'clock, and Jerry and Ben returned to their offices. Tiffany told Jerry that he'd had a call from Dave, who had asked Jerry to call him back as soon as possible. Jerry closed his door and returned Dave's call. "Well, you are the owner of twelve thousand shares of Optiscan. The final price was fifteen dollars per share, as we expected," Dave said. Again, every detail was precisely like Jerry's dream. Dave indicated he would fax him the confirmation. Dave thanked Jerry and again told him that this was going to be a very profitable investment.

Jackie arrived home from school about four and placed a call to the inn. She asked to speak with the owner, but since he was unavailable, she asked that he return her call when he had the chance. She also mentioned that they had stayed at the inn and had enjoyed their weekend.

Jackie started dinner, and the kids changed into their play clothes so they could romp in the snow before it got dark. At about five o'clock Jackie saw that the light was waning and called to the kids from the back door. As they bounded in, she reminded them to take off their wet boots and clothes and put them in the laundry room. After they got their wet things off, Jackie told them to start any homework they had.

Lisa didn't have any, but David had a science project due in a few days. Jackie tried to make sure they didn't let things go until the last minute.

She allowed Lisa to watch TV and had David begin his work in the kitchen so she could keep tabs on him. It was a cold day, and the night was expected to be in the low teens with a high wind. Jackie prepared some frozen beef stew that she had made several weeks earlier. She also decided to bake some brown-and-serve bread to go along with the stew. It was about six thirty when Jerry arrived home. Lisa and David greeted him at the door with big hugs.

Lisa said, "Don't forget to clean your boots and put your wet clothes in the laundry room, Dad."

"Yes, Mother," Jerry jokingly said. He knew she tried to imitate her mother about keeping the floor clean. Jerry asked them how school went, and they told him all the details of their day.

Jackie was pleased with the progress David was making on his science project and told him he could put it away and get washed for dinner. They all sat down, and Jackie served her homemade beef stew. When they finished dinner, the kids carried their plates to the sink and went into the family room to get ready to watch *Rudolph the Red-Nosed Reindeer.* Jackie and Jerry remained in the kitchen as they cleaned up the dishes.

"I talked with Dave just before leaving the office. He purchased the twelve thousand shares at fifteen dollars, just like in the dream. Now we'll have to wait until March to see if it all works out according to the dream."

Jackie asked him when in March he was to sell the shares. Jerry told her it was at the very end of March and the final selling price was eighty-eight dollars per share.

"I called the inn this afternoon, but the owner was unavailable. I asked him to please call me when he had a chance," said Jackie.

Not long after they finished the dishes the phone rang. Jackie was greeted by a friendly voice that identified the caller as Mr. Douglas, the owner of the Inn of Destiny. Jackie explained they had stayed there last

February, and she wanted to talk with other guests who had stayed in room D. Although agreeable, Mr. Douglas replied that he couldn't give out information about other guests. Jackie was a bit vague and only told him they'd had a unique time and wanted to share their experiences with others. Although she didn't mention their dreams, it was as though Mr. Douglas knew what she wanted.

"Are you aware of the history surrounding the inn?" Mr. Douglas asked.

"No. What history?"

He continued, "When the inn was being built, we discovered it was on an old Indian burial ground. As the excavation began, some human remains were uncovered along with some Indian artifacts. Work stopped until the extent of the burial ground was determined, and a second site was chosen next to the burial ground. There has been a lot of speculation by some of the guests about the bad karma from disturbing the burial site."

"Did anyone experience anything?" Jackie asked.

"Some of the early guests at the inn said they heard strange sounds like someone walking, and others claimed they saw a ghost that looked like an Indian chief with a headdress who was holding a tomahawk," answered Mr. Douglas.

"That sounds scary," remarked Jackie.

"We haven't heard of anyone seeing anything like that lately," he said. "I would like to help you, Mrs. French. The only thing I can suggest is that I will include a note from you in the newsletter we're getting ready to prepare. This letter goes to all our former guests, and if you can email me a short message, I'll see that it's included. In that way, you may be able to get in contact with some other guests that stayed in room D."

"Thank you, Mr. Douglas. I appreciate your suggestion. I'll send you an email tomorrow morning," Jackie said. She hung up and told Jerry what the owner had suggested.

They sat down and began to compose their note. They didn't want to make it sound like they were a couple of nuts. At the same time, they wanted to encourage anyone who may have had a similar experience to get in touch with them. They worked on the message while the kids watched *Rudolph*, and by the time the show was over, Jackie and Jerry had all but completed the message. They got the kids ready for bed, and after they were settled, Jackie decided to send the email that night. She knew how busy the mornings were and wanted to make sure Mr. Douglas had it for the newsletter.

About two weeks passed before the newsletter from the inn came in the mail. Jackie quickly looked for her letter. It was on the front page. Mr. Douglas had added a note encouraging other guests in room D to contact Jackie French. When Jerry arrived home, she showed him the newsletter. They both hoped this would enable them to see if others had had a similar unnerving experience. It would surely enhance their acceptance of the third dream if they learned they weren't the only guests to be given a glimpse into the future.

16

New Year's Eve

CHRISTMAS WAS A BUSY TIME in the French household, and this year was no exception. Jackie had all the normal preparations for her family as well as events at school. Her class was part of the school play, and the reception for parents was the last Tuesday before Christmas.

Christmas was good for most Americans, and this was certainly true for the French family. Everyone was well and the economy was the best in history. As for Jerry and Jackie, they both had successful careers and were living the good life. To top it off, their investments were outstanding, and the outlook was for more of the same.

Jackie and Jerry made a determined effort not to allow the potential impact of the market crash to spoil their holiday. They tried to put it out of their minds and enjoy the holiday season. Jackie did hope that she would get some responses from the article in the newsletter. However, she knew that most people had other things on their minds at this time of year. Jerry was able to keep track of Optiscan, and, as expected, it was increasing in price almost daily.

For the past several years Jackie and Mary had joined forces to host a New Year's Eve party. It had become one of the social events in Princeton. Having been started about ten years ago, the party had steadily grown to the point where it required a lot of planning and the efforts of both families. This year they decided to hold the party in both homes to accommodate the number of guests. To ensure that it was one party and not two celebrations, Mary suggested they consider renting a tent that would tie the two houses together. Jackie agreed, and Mary arranged to have a tent rental company come over to assess their needs.

It was early Saturday morning when Mary knocked at Jackie's back door. They had coffee, and about eight thirty Mr. Brown appeared at the front door. He looked at the homes and the back yards and listened to what they wanted to accomplish for the New Year's Eve party. He took some measurements and began to draw a sketch of the back yards. After a short time, he called to Mary and Jackie to look at his idea. The tent he proposed would connect the family rooms via their sliding doors. This would not only tie the two homes together but also provide a focal area for the party outside the actual homes. Both kitchens would be able to feed the party, and guests could enter from either front door. Mr. Brown suggested a dance floor to be placed in the middle of the tent, and he planned to locate a heater to the rear of the French yard. This would keep the noise at a minimum but make the tent comfortable.

Mary and Jackie liked the plan and decided to have Mr. Brown draw up the rental agreement. They also selected serving tables and decorations, including several potted plants. Mary suggested they locate the DJ in one corner and place the food around the edges on two sides of the tent. They would also use the living and family rooms in both houses for added space.

Most of the other details had long since been settled. The invitations were mailed in early fall. Many of the guests were regulars, and the invitation was only a formality. The food would make most caterers blush, but everything except the beverages was homemade by either Mary or Jackie. That was one of the things that made this party so special. The girls put themselves into it, and it showed. Despite its size, this wasn't another commercial affair. The husbands did the grunt work and made sure the ice, beverages, and furniture were on hand.

Given the size of the tent, Mary suggested she contact the temporary help company to see if they could get two more servers. They had arranged for two kitchen helpers and four servers. If they could add two servers, they would have six people circulating among the guests. As it turned out, the temp service was able to supply the additional help. Jackie and Mary had carefully planned the food to be served at this year's party. Each year they tried to introduce a few changes, although some things were annual favorites that couldn't be forgotten. It was almost noon when they finished reviewing the many details. "I guess I had better get moving," Mary said. They agreed to call each other if other questions came to mind.

Two days before New Year's Eve, the tent company arrived to set up the tent. It took four hours to set it up and install the heater. Mr. Brown was on the scene to supervise the work. He wanted to make sure his company did their part to make the couples' party a success. Jackie and Mary were pleased with the tent and thanked Mr. Brown and the workmen for their help. The crew would remove the tent on January 2, weather permitting.

After they left, the girls continued what seemed like an endless series of tasks to prepare the large number of culinary delights that awaited this year's guests. Some of the items had been made earlier and frozen. Other things had to be completed closer to the night of the party. Jerry and John had gone to a friend's to pick up another refrigerator as the girls were closing in on their final preparations. Finally, the guys arrived with the refrigerator. They were a welcome sight to Jackie since her kitchen resembled a large food storage room. Mary's kitchen was not much better. After the refrigerator was set up, Jerry and John began placing the food in it. Even after they completed this task, it seemed every cold-storage area was filled to capacity.

Jerry decided he had better call the icehouse since they were late in delivering the needed ice. He was assured that they were on their way and not to worry. At that, Jerry and John took John's truck and headed for the liquor store. They found that the beer and soft drinks were already cold, which simplified icing them down. The temperature was in the upper twenties, so the ice was in no danger of thawing. While the guys were at the beverage store, the ice finally arrived. Jackie showed the men where to place it, and in short order they completed this last and most important step. Jerry had set up a backup supply of ice at his parents' and several friends' homes. He would be glad to know they wouldn't be needed.

Jerry also had a backup for the DJ: a Wurlitzer jukebox in the family room that he planned to locate in the corner of the tent should the DJ fail to show up. That, too, was unneeded, as the DJ arrived soon after the ice delivery was completed to set up and test his equipment. By the time the guys returned from getting the beverages, everything was ready. All that was needed now were the guests. The weather was clear but cold, so Jerry cranked up the tent heaters soon after he returned home.

The party was to begin at nine thirty, and the servers and kitchen help were to arrive at eight thirty. By seven o'clock, the two couples decided that everything was in order and it was time to get dressed. Mary and John left for their house, and Jackie and Jerry headed upstairs. Jerry shaved and got into the shower. Jackie got undressed and decided that she would start the evening's festivities off a little early. She stepped in the shower with Jerry and decided he needed some help washing his package. Jerry's face showed how great Jackie was at sex.

She knew just how hard to squeeze it to make Jerry lose himself in the pleasure. After she was sure it was clean, she decided it was time for another of her specialties—oral sex. Those twenty minutes got the night off to what would prove to be an outstanding celebration that would last until the sun came up the next morning.

It was just about eight thirty when Jackie finished getting dressed. Jerry was already downstairs waiting for Mary and John. Jackie made her grand entrance in a striking red silk dress. She looked elegant, showing just a hint of the fantastic body she had under that silk. Jerry was a bit taken aback and told her how truly beautiful she was. Just as Jackie got to the kitchen, Mary arrived. John had remained at their house to finish a few things and wait for the help that would be working out of his house. The help arrived about twenty of nine, and Mary took one of the kitchen helpers and three servers to her house. The girls had tried to split things up evenly to help make sure this was truly one celebration.

About nine o'clock the DJ arrived. He had set up everything earlier and only had to turn on the equipment and practice a few minutes. They were off and running about twenty after nine before the first guests arrived. After giving the help their final instructions, the two couples went to their front doors to greet the guests.

The homes and the tent were outstanding. The Christmas decorations in the two houses made it clear these were two couples that did everything with class. The tent was decorated for the New Year with a large banner. There were potted plants placed throughout the tent, and the serving tables were placed to provide convenient access to the food and beverages without interfering with the dance floor.

The selection of the food included peeled shrimp, oysters Rockefeller, imported and domestic cheeses, liver pâté, caviar, buffalo wings, sesame chicken strips, assorted fruits and vegetables, several types of dip and crackers, deviled eggs, pasta salad, potato salad, pizza squares, and a Swiss cheese fondue with French bread. The desserts were equally impressive and included assorted petit fours, pies, and cakes. There was also a chocolate dessert fondue with fresh fruit. The bar was stocked with every imaginable type of hard and soft drink. There were cases of champagne to celebrate the New Year in a fitting way. Coffee and tea were also available to round out the offerings.

It was just after nine thirty when the first guest got to the Frenches' home. After that, there was a steady stream of arrivals through about half past ten, when all of the guests had arrived. The party was a big success. The guests loved the idea of combining the two homes, and the tent with the dance floor. And the DJ was the thing that made it really work. The food and beverages continued throughout the evening. The dance floor was never vacant. The DJ took only a ten-minute break, as he sensed how much the guests liked the music. It was about ten minutes before midnight when the TV sets were turned on to prepare for the big event. The familiar scene at Times Square blared throughout the tent and family rooms.

Everyone was served a glass of champagne as the ball began its inevitable descent to the bottom of the long pole. As the seconds ticked off, all were ready to do their part to greet the New Year. At the stroke of midnight, the guests sang out with "Happy New Year!" As soon as the merriment of that moment was past, the DJ returned to playing and everyone began dancing with their partners. There were couples dancing in the family rooms and living rooms and on the dance floor in the tent.

After another twenty minutes of dancing, the crowd seemed to have worked up a fresh appetite and the food and beverages again took center stage. About twelve thirty, Jerry went over to the DJ and asked him if he would stay until 2:00 a.m. He agreed, and Jerry handed him three hundred dollars as a bonus.

The music ended at two o'clock, and gradually people began to leave. By two thirty, the DJ had packed up and left, and the last of the guests walked out the door. The help did a great job of cleaning up and stacking the mounds of refuse in plastic bags behind the garage. The help was finished about a quarter of three, and they, too, said good night. Jackie and Mary were hyped up from the evening.

17

The Dreams of Others

ALTHOUGH IT WAS ALMOST 3:00 A.M., they weren't ready to end the festivities. Jackie got one of those looks on her face, and Mary wanted to know what was on her mind. "Let us start our sex life this year with something different," said Jackie. Mary was almost afraid to hear what Jackie had come up with now.

"What do you want to do? Have an orgy?" asked Mary.

Jackie leaned over and suggested they exchange beds for the night. "I'll go over and crawl under the covers with John, and you entertain Jerry." Jackie suggested they try to keep their husbands from learning of the switch until they were well along the path to ecstasy.

Mary thought for a minute and said, "Let's do it." She told John to go home, get into bed, and turn out the lights. She told him to pretend he was asleep and see what would happen. Jackie told Jerry the same thing. Both husbands were quick to cooperate, as they anticipated some great sex. Little did they know what was really in store for them that early New Year's morning.

Jackie went over to Mary's and took off her clothes outside the bedroom door. She slowly opened the door of the darkened room and quickly slid under the covers with John. Mary took her clothes off in Jackie's kitchen and went up to Jerry, who was pretending to be asleep.

Mary was also successful in sneaking under the covers without Jerry suspecting anything.

Jackie knew that John was very close to the top, and she decided to let him know that it wasn't Mary giving him this pleasure. She gently pulled the covers down. There was just enough light in the room for John to see that it was Jackie in his bed. At first, John began to sit up but soon realized what the girls had cooked up. He allowed Jackie to finish the job without saying a word.

Mary continued working on Jerry until he exploded. After he finished, she came out from under the covers and asked what he thought of the first round. Jerry was dumfounded. There had never been any hint of wife swapping. He was so turned on by what he had just learned, he began to kiss Mary and proceeded to give Mary her moment of pleasure. Jerry was as good a lover as Jackie said he was, and Mary decided this was indeed a great end to the New Year's celebration.

Things were about the same in Mary's bed. Jackie was being treated to some outstanding sex. John kissed Jackie and gave her a great deal of pleasure. It wasn't long before Jackie screamed with delight, as John was successful in pleasing her. Jackie got on top of John and was pleased at how quickly she could bring him into submission.

Mary and Jerry continued their lovemaking until almost 5:00 a.m. Jackie and John didn't stop until six. The girls had agreed to return home at eight thirty, and they passed each other in the tent on their way back to their own husbands. When the men got up, nothing was said about what had taken place that early New Year's morning. It was as if they all knew this was a onetime fling and was as much a part of the fantastic party as anything. Both couples were very much in love with their spouses, and this was just a unique way to get the New Year off to a fast start. By noon, Mary and John were showered and dressed, heading to his parents' for a New Year's Day dinner. It took Jackie and Jerry a little longer to head for Jackie's parents' and their New Year's Day celebration.

The New Year was in its infancy when events surrounding their dreams began to cascade upon them. First of all, Optiscan kept going higher and higher in price. By mid-January, it had already reached thirty-five dollars per share. Second, Jackie had four calls on the answering machine. She copied the messages down and decided to call one woman, Mrs. Mann, who seemed anxious to talk with her about their stay at the inn. Jackie decided to return her call first, and after dinner she asked Jerry if he wanted to get on the extension while she called her. Jackie dialed the number, and in just a few rings a woman answered: "Hello? This is Joan Mann. How may I help you?"

Jackie answered, "This is Jackie French returning your call. My husband, Jerry, is on the extension. We want to thank you for responding to our note in the newsletter."

"I assume you had an unusual experience when you stayed at the inn," Mrs. Mann said.

"Yes, we sure did," Jackie responded. She asked Mrs. Mann when they had been guests and if they'd stayed in the same room.

Mrs. Mann told her, "Two years ago my husband and I spent a December weekend in room D. I was the one that had the dream, and it proved to be a life-altering experience."

Mrs. Mann went into more detail as she told them about the dream she'd had on that Friday night. She said she saw an automobile accident that resulted in the death of their only child. They were only going a short distance to the corner convenience store, and her daughter didn't use her seat belt. A dump truck came out of nowhere and struck the right front of their car. She explained that her car was older and didn't have an airbag on the passenger side. Her daughter went through the windshield and was killed instantly. "I woke up and was so upset by the reality of the dream that I woke my husband out of a sound sleep. He calmed me down and reminded me that it was only a dream. It took me over an hour to get back to sleep, and it haunted me for weeks after our trip."

Mrs. Mann told them that about six months later, she and her daughter were on their way to the convenience store, and she looked over to see that Donna didn't have her seat belt fastened. At that moment she remembered that horrible dream. Immediately she told Donna to fasten her belt, and Donna did so. Less than two blocks later a large dump truck struck them in the right front. Her car was seriously damaged, but no one was injured. "When I looked at the car it was exactly like it had looked in my dream. The truck was the same, and even the driver seemed familiar. The only difference was that my daughter was fine."

When they got home, she had told her husband about her dream and how it had saved Donna's life. "I often wondered why I had the dream. I didn't associate it with the inn until I read your note in the newsletter. Have you talked with anyone else who had a dream at the inn that came true?"

Jackie answered, "No. Not yet. You are the first call I returned. I do have three other calls to answer."

"If it isn't too personal, what was your dream about?" Mrs. Mann asked.

"Well," answered Jackie, "my husband had three separate dreams on Saturday night, and I had one dream on Friday. My dream was very personal, but I can tell you that my experience and my recalling the dream prevented a very serious incident from taking place. In that respect, you and I are similar. My husband's dreams were about investments. His first dream was about an investment that he didn't make that was shown to be an error in the dream. In that same dream, he was also shown a second investment that he did buy and made a lot of money from, just as his dream predicted."

Jackie continued, "Everything in his first dream came true. Just like yours, every detail was accurate. He invested in another stock and purchased it the same as in his second dream. To date, it's responding like it did in the dream. The real dilemma is the third dream, which depicts an event that won't take place for over a year. We don't know if this will come to pass, but if it does, it will have a catastrophic impact on us and our families."

"I can see your dilemma. With my dream it was once and done. The only thing we had to reconcile was how it saved our daughter's life. I don't know what I would do if I were in your situation. I can understand why you're trying to contact others," Mrs. Mann said.

At the end of their conversation, they exchanged information, including email addresses, and promised to keep in touch.

"Well, that surely lends credence to my dream," Jerry said.

"I can't wait to see if we can uncover any other people who can duplicate the experience we and the Manns had at the inn," Jackie responded.

It was time for the kids to get ready for bed. After they were tucked in, Jackie placed a call to a Mrs. Johnson who had said she lived in Indiana and stayed at the inn last winter. The phone rang several times before a male voice answered, "Hello?"

"Is Mrs. Johnson available?" Jackie asked.

"Yes. Who shall I say is calling?"

"It's Jackie French returning her call."

"Just a minute, please."

Jackie motioned to Jerry to pick up the other phone.

"Hello. This is Irene Johnson."

"Hi, I'm Jackie French. You left a message on my answering machine in response to my note in the newsletter from the Inn of Destiny. My husband, Jerry, is on the extension." Jackie explained that she was attempting to contact other guests who had stayed at the inn.

"I take it you've been having some unexplained events in your life that you dreamed about while staying at the inn," Mrs. Johnson said.

"We sure have. Both my husband and I had dreams that are coming true," Jackie explained.

"Did you stay in room D?" Mrs. Johnson inquired.

"Yes."

Mrs. Johnson described the dream she'd had about her son being admitted to a particular medical school. Her husband had also had a dream about a serious problem with a partnership he was part of in Indianapolis. In both cases, everything had turned out the same as in their dreams.

Jackie explained that she'd had one dream that changed her actions based on what the dream indicated would take place. She also told Mrs. Johnson about Jerry's dreams and how one of them was only partially complete, while the third dream was over a year in the future. She also told her about the conversation she had just completed with Joan Mann. Jackie didn't tell Mrs. Johnson Mrs. Mann's name, but did describe her dream in general terms.

After about an hour, Jackie and Irene agreed to keep in touch, and they exchanged addresses. Mrs. Johnson didn't have an email address and didn't seem to be into computers. She seemed much older than Mrs. Mann and Jackie. Jackie guessed Irene was in her early sixties.

After this call it was late, and Jackie and Jerry decided to call it a day. They would try to call the other two people who had left messages the following night. At this point, there was little doubt in their minds that they had been given a look into the future. Not once but on four separate occasions. They went to bed and had a hard time falling asleep. They were anxious to hear what the other two guests had to report about the inn.

The next morning finally arrived. Both Jackie and Jerry were tired because they hadn't got very much sleep. However, Jerry got the old 7:20, and Jackie drove the kids to school as usual. Lisa and David attended the same school where Jackie taught, but they weren't in her class. The school tried to avoid having children in their parent's classroom. The day seemed to fly by, and it wasn't long before the dismissal bell rang.

As soon as the kids got out of the car, they changed into their play clothes so they could go out in the snow before dark. Jackie started dinner, and Jerry arrived home after six as usual. After dinner, the kids had some homework they hadn't done due to playing in the snow.

Jackie supervised their work and Jerry turned on the news. After the kids completed their work, they wanted to play a family game, and the four of them played Old Maid. Lisa especially liked that game, and it was something they could all play. After their game, the kids got their baths and went to bed.

Jackie said, "Let's try to reach the other two people."

"Fine," Jerry responded.

The first number Jackie called was busy. She tried the last caller, and after a few rings a man answered. As it turned out, he was unable to confirm any dreams or anything unusual. He did tell Jackie that they had stayed in room D, but that was all. Jackie didn't go into the dreams because she didn't want him to think she was some kind of nut. It was different if the other guest had had a dream that came true. In this case, she thanked him and hung up.

Jackie then tried the number that had been busy before, and it began to ring. The woman who answered said, "This is Mrs. Bray."

"Hello. I'm Jackie French. You returned my call the other day."

"Oh, yes. What can I do for you?" she asked. Jackie had started to explain about the dreams when Mrs. Bray said, "I wondered if we were the only one. I guess your call proves there are others." She told Jackie about the dream her husband had had in which his assistant was promoted and became his boss in the end. As it turned out, events at Mr. Bray's job had made him think that his dream was coming true.

Jackie relayed the dreams that she and Jerry had had and told her about the other two people she had talked with who'd had similar experiences. Like with the other two, they exchanged addresses and said they would keep in touch. It was as if they had formed a small club of futurists.

After they completed their calls, Jerry turned to Jackie and said, "Now what? It seems everyone who had a dream that came true didn't have our problem. We seem to be the only ones with multiple dreams, and the question is, Will the last one come true?"

"Do you have any doubt that the market will crash?" Jackie asked.

"Not much. If Optiscan falls into place by the end of March, I think we must act to protect ourselves. Now we must decide how to share this information with our family and close friends. April seems a long way off. However, it will come, and we will need to be prepared."

18

The Decision

FRIDAY WAS A TYPICAL WEEKDAY at the Frenches' and brought with it the expected daily activities. Jerry decided to have a bowl of oatmeal for breakfast to help him prepare for a busy day at the office. He was about ready to finalize the negotiations for the major acquisitions his firm was considering. In addition, the matter of what to do about his last dream weighed heavily on his mind. He wanted some closure, at least, as to how he would protect his family and let his close friends know of this possibility.

After Jerry finished his breakfast, he said to Jackie, "We need to decide what to do about the dream and how to discuss it with others. Let's set aside some time this weekend to see if you and I can come up with an answer that makes sense to us."

"I agree. This is constantly overshadowing everything for me," Jackie responded.

"You have a good day at school," Jerry told Jackie and the kids. "I'll see you tonight." He kissed them, got into his car, and drove to the station. Jackie finished the dishes and got the kids ready to leave for school.

Friday was an uneventful day compared with the last several weeks, and soon Jackie and the kids were home for the weekend and Jerry was coming in the back door from New York. They decided to go out for dinner and ended up at Friendly's. The kids loved this since they could eat ice cream anytime. It didn't matter that the weather was cold enough to store the ice cream outside. After they returned home, the kids wanted to see a new video, and Jerry and Jackie began dealing with their dreams. Although they talked until the kids went to bed, they were no closer to an answer than before they started.

Lisa and David were going to a sleepover party Saturday, and they were full of it starting early in the morning. Jackie had a short list of things for them to do, and they quickly completed their chores. After lunch, Jerry drove them to their friend's house for the party.

Jackie and Jerry got started as soon as he got home from dropping the kids off. They considered a number of options, from just treating it like it wouldn't take place to alerting a large number of their friends. By early evening, they still hadn't settled on a solution. Then an expression came over Jerry's face that said to Jackie that he had an idea. He had, in fact, come to a decision, but he wanted to make sure she agreed with it.

Jackie said, "It looks as if you've come up with something."

Jerry proceeded to lay out his plan. First, he didn't want to get into Jackie's dream due to its personal nature. After all, her dream didn't have any significance on the market crash issue except to help convince them this dream thing was more than a fluke.

Jerry proposed to prepare two sets of envelopes that they would use to inform Dave and their close friends Mary and John about the dreams. The first envelope would explain the first two of Jerry's dreams and how they had started to come true. It would include the upshot of the Optiscan investment at the end of March. In that way, when March dawned, the predictions in the first envelope would help prepare the way for the revelation about the market crash, which would be outlined in detail in the second envelope.

The instructions would be to open the first envelope before the end of March. The second envelope should be opened after the results of the Optiscan investment were known. As far as the issue with their parents, Jerry was already managing their retirement accounts. He suggested that, rather than get them upset about the world crisis, he would just move their assets into areas that wouldn't be impacted by the market crash.

Jackie listened with amazement to what her husband was saying. She realized that he had compassion and a degree of wisdom that surpassed anyone else she knew. When he finished, Jackie said to him, "I think your plan is excellent. I knew you'd be able to deal with this unusual situation. I'm proud of you, dear."

Jerry was glad that Jackie agreed so strongly with his plan. They spent the remainder of the evening writing the two letters that they would give to their friends. When they had completed the actual letters, they briefly talked about the ways they might protect themselves. The good thing was they had more than a year to prepare for this crash. In addition, there was a strong possibility that if their friends believed this was to happen, they would be able to work as a team to develop the exact way to both defend against loss and turn this crash into the final step in their own financial destiny. Little did Jackie know when she made the reservation that she had ushered in one of the most significant events of their life! Who would have guessed a simple weekend at the inn might be the porthole to the future!

19

The Dinner Party

ON SUNDAY, they turned to the question of how they would give the envelopes to their friends. Jerry was not in favor of just giving these bombshells to them without talking about them. Jackie agreed and suggested they invite the two couples to an adult dinner party. They planned to give the first sealed envelopes to them prior to the party and ask each couple to bring it with them unopened. After their dinner, Jackie and Jerry would ask them to open their envelopes and read the contents for the first time. After that, they would be able to discuss what they just learned. At the conclusion of the evening, Jackie and Jerry would give them each the second sealed envelope and ask them to return about the first of May, when they would repeat the process and discuss Jerry's last dream. Jerry planned to tell them that the second envelope contained a prediction of an event that would take place in April. In that way, the two couples would be somewhat prepared for their second meeting.

Jackie looked at the calendar and thought the best date for the dinner party was the third Saturday in March. This would be just before the final events surrounding Optiscan were known. However, since they would have the envelope prior to the dinner, and the letter from Jackie and Jerry was dated February 1, there would be no question as to the predictions from the first dream. As a result, it would help them accept the events depicted in Jerry's second dream. Jackie contacted Mary first and confirmed that would be a good date for them. She called Alice, Dave's wife, to see if they were available on the twentieth. As it turned out, that was fine with them. After they both confirmed the date, Jerry took Dave's envelope to work and handed it to him over lunch.

Dave was most intrigued by what might be in this mysterious envelope. After all, this wasn't the usual way to deliver a formal invitation to dinner. When Jackie gave Mary her envelope, she wanted to open it. Jackie asked her to please be patient. She told her that Dave and Alice would be joining them, and that they, too, had received a sealed envelope.

…

Jackie called Mary as soon as she got home from school. She went over to Mary's house before her kids returned home, to get the latest news on Mary's morning exercise. Mary went over every detail and suggested that Jackie might like to give Paul a try. Jackie declined and told Mary size wasn't everything. Besides, she'd had her fling with a big stud while in high school. Mary had to admit that even Paul's huge tool didn't bring her to climax. It still took manual stimulation to get the job done properly.

Several weeks passed after Mary's Friday adventure, and it was only a week before Jackie's party. Jackie sent a little reminder saying, "Don't forget your envelope. It's your ticket for dinner." After Mary and Alice got Jackie's notes, they called to again try to learn what was up with the envelopes. Jackie told them both, "You will find out Saturday night after dinner. Be prepared for something like nothing you've ever experienced before in your life!"

Jackie went all out to plan a dinner that would be up to the task at hand. She would begin with some hors d'oeuvres, followed by a salad containing exotic fruits and vegetables. The main course was a standing rib roast with twice-baked potatoes and several steamed vegetables. Jackie made crescent rolls with honey whipped butter and served a red wine with the dinner. For dessert, she made a lemon meringue pie and planned to have several types of coffee and tea. This would be followed by an after-dinner drink.

It was about seven o'clock when Dave and Alice arrived, followed shortly after by Mary and John. Both couples had their envelopes and wanted to open them as soon as they were seated in the living room. Jackie asked them to please be patient until after dinner. They agreed, and Jackie went to the kitchen for the hors d'oeuvres while Jerry took their drink orders. The dinner was a smashing success, and they managed to keep the conversation on other subjects throughout the meal. The girls cleared the table after they were finished with dessert, and the three men retired to the den for an after-dinner drink.

It was about nine thirty when the ladies rejoined them. Jerry stood up and said, "The time has come to share something with you that may change all of our lives. I want you to know the decision to share the information in the envelopes wasn't easy. We will give you time to read the letter Jackie and I have written to you. After you've had a chance to let it settle in a bit, we'll return and discuss it with you. At the end of this evening, we have a second sealed envelope that we ask you not to open until we meet again in April, when we plan to do this all over again."

Jackie and Jerry went to the kitchen to finish cleaning up the dinner dishes while their friends read their letters. In about twenty minutes, Jackie and Jerry returned to their friends, who sat in their chairs with expressions of amazement on their faces. "Just wait until you open the second envelope in April," Jerry told them. What followed was the most astonishing discussion they ever had together. In fact, it was probably one of the most bizarre conversations of all times.

The couples decided to meet on the first Saturday in April to open the second letters, which Jerry handed them as they left. He asked them not to open these before their next dinner. Everyone agreed, and they said good night.

"I wonder what the conversations will be tonight in our friends' bedrooms," Jackie said.

Jerry replied, "I would love to be a fly on the wall."

20

The Second Letter

Time flew by, and as predicted in Jerry's dream, by the end of March the price of Optiscan rose and the investment made Jackie and Jerry almost $750,000.

Before long it was that all-important Saturday evening. The two couples were a few minutes early, which demonstrated the anticipation in the air. Jerry asked if they would like something to drink, but everyone just wanted to open their second envelopes.

They proceeded to open the envelopes, and as they read the contents, expressions of disbelief replaced their earlier expressions of anticipation. Dave was the first to speak. "I don't understand how this is possible, but I know the business about the IPOs is for real."

Jackie began to tell them about the similar experiences other guests in room D had had over the years. She didn't discuss her dream about Chris, although Mary was well aware of it. It was clear from the conversation that followed that everyone accepted Jerry's dreams as bizarre but true.

The conversation then turned to the Middle East conflict. The men agreed that such an incident was not so hard to believe. Most of them had some knowledge of the conflicts in the past and were aware of the current stalemate in the peace process.

Dave said, "I, for one, think we should take Jerry's dream as a warning and develop a plan to protect our investments in the event the last dream is true." The others agreed that the worst that could happen if the Middle East conflict didn't develop was that they would have repositioned their investments for a time.

After several hours of intense discussion, they agreed to begin laying out plans to protect themselves. As the investment expert, Dave would lead the way in providing some alternatives. They agreed to get together and review the options Dave had to offer.

Jerry asked that they limit their discussion with others, but acknowledged they may want to look after their families' investments. He did wonder how Dave would be able to keep this information confidential and still do what he thought was best for his clients.

It was about eleven thirty when they decided to call it a night. The next year would prove to be a time of great anticipation as they prepared to meet the potential challenge that might come into their lives.

21

The Investment Plans

Dave was familiar with Jerry's investments, but to make sure he had included everything, he provided Jerry with a list of his holdings for his review. Dave met with John in early May to obtain a list of his investments. Dave wanted to present several options, as well as to make specific recommendations for Jerry and John since their investments were somewhat different.

Dave had reached a point where he wanted to talk about his overall concept with Jerry. Since they both worked in the city, Dave decided to call Jerry and see if he was free for lunch. As it turned out, a lunch meeting Jerry had scheduled had been canceled and he was available. Dave suggested a quiet café near their offices where they could talk in private. They agreed to meet at noon.

Dave arrived just before noon, and Jerry joined him a few minutes later. Dave asked the waiter to seat them in a rear corner booth so they could talk in private. They both ordered sandwiches, and Dave removed a tablet from his briefcase to take notes.

"Did you review the list of your investments I sent?" Dave asked.

"Yes. They look complete," Jerry replied.

"I plan to call John in a few days to see if he's received the list I prepared for him," said Dave. "I've developed three plans for us to consider.

I'd like your gut feeling and to see if you have any other concepts that I should develop."

The first plan simply moved their assets into money market investments. For IRA-type investments, Dave suggested creating a self-directed IRA account to hold the proceeds using a direct rollover. This would avoid any adverse tax effects of the investment changes. This plan would offer a safe harbor until the crisis was over. There was a low risk of market fluctuation, and the investments would earn the rate the money market accounts were paying at the time.

The second plan would be to convert their assets to gold during the period of the downturn. This option held the possibility to realize capital appreciation if the price of gold increased because of the crisis in the Middle East. It, too, was a safe hedge against a loss and had the possibility of some gain during the crisis.

The third plan would be to convert IRA assets to a safe harbor, similar to the other two plans, and sell the after-tax investments to fund the required margin for the short sale of stocks that would be expected to drop in price during the crash. When the price of the securities that were sold fell short and a temporary bottom, or lull, took place, the short sales would be covered and the profits invested in a safe-harbor investment to protect the gain.

Jerry suggested that when they considered the best option for each family, they might use portions of all three plans. Dave agreed and pointed out that the plan for their parents' assets could be very different from their own plan. They agreed to have a meeting of the six adults and try to develop more specific plans for each situation. Jerry said, "I'll ask Jackie to set up dinner at our house within the next several weeks."

"That sounds fine," Dave replied. They finished their lunch and headed back to their offices.

That evening Jerry told Jackie about his meeting with Dave. She agreed to call the wives to set up another dinner meeting. Jerry suggested the end of June to give Dave time to get his plans prepared.

Jackie called Mary later that evening to see what would fit her calendar, and Mary suggested they have the dinner meeting at her house on the last Saturday in June. Jackie agreed and told Mary she would call Alice to see if that met with their schedule.

When Jackie finished the dinner dishes and got the kids settled, she called Alice. Dave answered, and Jackie asked him if that was OK with them to review the investment options. He took a minute to talk with Alice and confirmed that would be fine. Jackie told him the meeting would be next door at Mary and John's home at 8:00 p.m. He asked if they should bring anything. Jackie responded, "Just some good ideas."

22

Planning to Weather the Storm

MARY DECIDED TO HAVE A BARBECUE and set up the patio for dinner. She decided on porterhouse steaks, twice-baked potatoes, green beans, and a salad. Dessert would be her homemade Key lime pie. Jackie came over about seven o'clock to help her friend get set for dinner. Jerry and John had been playing golf and arrived home about seven thirty. Dave and Alice were a bit late due to a problem they'd had with their babysitter. They rang the doorbell about eight fifteen. The couples decided to have drinks before dinner and begin reviewing the plans Dave prepared after they finished dinner.

The meal was a great success and a perfect lead-in to the important discussion that followed. Dave had made copies of the three plans he had reviewed with Jerry, and they all agreed to take them home and get back to him when they had made their decisions for their own investments as well as for their family members. The meeting lasted about two hours, and Dave and Alice were the first to leave. Jerry and Jackie helped clean up and went home about eleven thirty.

Jerry and John decided to work together on their plans. They also agreed not to reveal the details of the predictions to their parents and in-laws. After all, most of their assets were already in more stable income-producing investments, and there was no reason to upset them about the impending crisis. They decided to suggest further movement of their assets to money market funds prior to the predicted market crash.

It was time to consider their own plans, and Jerry suggested they use parts of the three approaches Dave had described. They agreed and began making specific outlines. Jerry was a bit more aggressive than John and decided to convert his IRAs and 401(k) investments to money market funds. In some cases, it would mean just changing from one fund to another within the same fund manager. In other cases, he would use a self-directed IRA to convert the investments to money market accounts without affecting his taxes. For his after-tax investments, Jerry proposed to invest in gold and use the short-sale option to take advantage of the expected drop in the market as a result of the crisis. He decided to move 40 percent of his after-tax investments to gold and convert the remaining 60 percent to available funds in his brokerage accounts to meet the margin requirements of the short sales. He would seek Dave's advice on the exact timing of the gold purchase as well as the stocks to be used for the short sales. Although most stocks would most likely experience some price drop, the trick was to select those that would experience the greatest percentage drop. That would require a detailed knowledge of the stocks and the market just prior to the crash.

John's plan was the same for his before-tax investments, such as his IRAs, but he decided to split his after-tax investments in thirds. The first third would be converted to money market funds, the second third to gold, and the final third to short sales. He, too, would seek Dave's advice on the timing and the stocks to be used for the short sales.

After they completed their outlines, Jerry suggested they call Dave to see if he was available for a videoconference. Jerry had installed this feature on his PC and thought it was an effective communication tool. John thought that was a good idea, and Jerry proceeded to call Dave. As it turned out, Dave was also considering his options and agreed to fire up his PC so they could have their videoconference.

It took a few minutes to get set up, and they began reviewing the two plans with Dave. He thought the plans were sound and agreed to act as their broker to implement their plans when the time was right. He told them he would begin sending them a list of potential short-sell stocks.

The summer passed quickly, and it wasn't long before the cool nights signaled the onset of fall. It was peaceful both in world politics and on Wall Street. It was hard to believe that within six months the events in Jerry's dream could take place. Dave conferred with Jerry and John, and as December arrived, he began sending possible short-sale stocks for them to consider.

In January there was a flurry of activity between the Palestinian Authority and Israel on a peace agreement. This process was viewed by some of the more radical elements in the Palestinian movement as a move to weaken the support for their demands for a separate state. This sparked a series of incidents between the Palestinians and the Israelis that ended with the death of several hundred people and massive demonstrations throughout the Middle East. The unrest was so serious that even countries like Egypt and Saudi Arabia condemned the violence. They were especially critical of the level of force used by the Israelis. News of this spread like wildfire, and the president and European leaders were frantic to restore order to avoid what could become an all-consuming conflict. Stock markets all over the world reacted negatively to the events, and Wall Street experienced broad-based drops that ranged from 25 percent in the DOW to over 40 percent in the NASDAQ.

Although they had been planning to weather the storm, these events still troubled the three men. Had they misread the timing? Could all their planning have been for nothing? In the end, the president was able to forge a cease-fire that stopped the killing on both sides and got the two sides to agree to resume peace talks. By the first week in February, the financial markets recovered and the averages returned to just below their precrisis levels. For Jerry, John, and Dave, this scare only made them more certain that the predictions in Jerry's dream were about to unfold.

23

The Prophesy

BY THE FIRST OF MARCH, the men's levels of anxiety were beginning to increase as the time for implementing their plans drew near. It was one thing to put a plan on paper and quite another to put it in place.

Though all three men had difficulty not showing the effects of their foreknowledge in their daily lives, Dave was affected the most because he knew how the expected events would affect his clients. In fact, implementing his own investment shifts had to be carefully considered. He couldn't appear to be in possession of information on what was about to happen. It was a bit different from insider information of securities, however. Who would believe that anyone could know about an event like this? Nevertheless, Dave decided not to use the short-sale option and chose to use money market funds and gold. He had always thought that gold was ready for a move and would use this as a pretext for this shift. As for the use of money market funds, he wanted to reposition some of his investments and chose them as a temporary resting place until he purchased his new securities.

The first accounts to be changed were the retirement funds for their parents. This was rather simple, and there was no problem convincing their parents to buy the money market funds. After these accounts were converted, Jerry began to move his assets per his plan, and the cash balance in his brokerage account began to skyrocket. By the end of March, Dave and John had completed their plans, and Jerry was almost finished with a slightly altered plan. Jerry decided on 40 percent in gold, 50 percent for short sales, and the remaining 10 percent in money market accounts. The only steps that remained were the actual purchase of the gold and to complete the short sales.

Dave provided the final list of stocks he recommended for their short sales and advised them to buy the gold on April 5. He began to complete the short sales April 11 and placed the last short-sale transaction on the twelfth. By the close of business on the twelfth, the purchases and short sales were confirmed, and Dave faxed copies to Jerry and John.

At 10:00 a.m., a broadcast alert sounded followed by a bulletin crossing television screens. It said that at 10:30 a.m. est there was to be an announcement by a spokesperson representing OPEC and the Palestinian Authority. No other explanation was given, but this set off a round of speculation by the newscasters as to what this meant.

For the past several weeks, the news coming from the Middle East had been that the peace talks were expected to end without a resolution because of the same key issues that had prevented all other accords: the Palestinian state, the status of East Jerusalem, return of four million Palestinians to their former homes in Israel, the Jewish settlements, and the security of Israel. For a time, there did appear to be some movement on Israeli security, the four million Palestinians, and the outline of what would constitute the new Palestinian state. However, the question of East Jerusalem and control of the holy sites eluded agreement.

At 10:20, there were reports of new clashes between the Palestinian police and Israeli soldiers. The level of speculation rose as rumors that numerous heads of state from OPEC would be at the announcement. Jerry and John could not believe their eyes. Although they'd both said they expected the predictions in the dream to be true, there was always some doubt that it would actually take place. At that moment, the phone rang. It was John making sure Jerry was watching the events on

TV. At exactly ten thirty the news on all major channels turned to the announcement that was about to be made.

A spokesman dressed in an Islamic robe stood at the podium surrounded by most of the heads of state that made up OPEC. Never before had this group been assembled to make an announcement. The representative took out a prepared statement, and the words that followed were the worst nightmare of both diplomats and industrial leaders throughout the world.

"An agreement has been reached between the OPEC nations and the Palestinian Authority to support the formation of a Palestinian state with its capital in East Jerusalem. Too long have the Palestinian people been denied a country of their own. If such an agreement is not signed by May 1, a unilateral declaration of statehood will be enacted. If the implementation and operation of the new Palestinian state is prevented by Israel, OPEC will suspend all oil shipments to the West until there is the full and complete cooperation by Israel and all other interested parties."

At that, the group left the news conference without answering any questions. For the next few seconds there was dead air on the news networks.

The next announcement was that the president would address the nation. Reports were now circulating that the White House had learned of the announcement at 9:00 a.m. The next scene was the familiar Seal of the President followed by his entrance behind the podium. He proceeded to tell the American people that he had been informed about the announcement and provided with a copy of the statement that morning. He was unable to speak with the OPEC leaders prior to their announcement. He further explained that he had contacted the Israeli prime minister to advise him of the announcement. The prime minister had informed the president that he, too, had been given a copy of the statement at the same time the president had received his copy. The president wanted to assure everyone that nothing would be a higher priority than attempting to find a solution to this situation. He didn't take questions and left the podium at the conclusion of his statement.

By then, it was about 11:10 and their attention turned to their PCs and the market. Just as in Jerry's dream, all hell was breaking loose in the markets. By 1:00 p.m., there was an announcement that the exchanges would close at two o'clock. Everything was unfolding the same as it had in the dream. The only difference was that Jerry wasn't on the golf course, but he was with his boss.

The phone rang. It was Jackie.

"Have you been watching?" she asked. Her school had put the news on the TV system in the building. Except for Jackie, everyone stood dumbfounded.

The hope was that over the weekend something could be done to avert a potential disaster in the Middle East. Israel reacted with threats of military action should the level of violence increase or if the Palestinians were to try to occupy the areas included in the new Palestinian state.

John and Jerry just stared at each other in disbelief. *How and why were we given this window to the future?* Although they were glad they had protected themselves, they couldn't help but wonder how many people would be hurt before this was over.

John said, "I wish your dream had lasted a bit longer so we would know the outcome of this crisis."

Jerry responded, "Did you ever hear of the saying, 'Be careful what you ask for'?"

Friday fulfilled the remainder of the dream's predictions, and the markets were closed from 2:00 p.m. Friday until Tuesday to help restore order. In the week that followed Jerry, John, and Dave completed their investment plans and consolidated their gains into safe-harbor investments to wait out the Middle East crisis.

Jerry not only had protected his investments but also had a gain of 250 percent over his precrisis holdings. John was a bit more conservative but did achieve a 200 percent profit. Dave achieved a gain of 40 percent since he didn't opt for short selling, and his gain came from the increased price of gold.

There was an unprecedented diplomatic effort by all world leaders to avert the crisis from starting a war. By May 1, face-to-face negotiations were underway between Israel and the Palestinians that were beginning to show real progress. It appeared that coming to the brink of disaster had enabled both sides to approach a solution with more flexibility and an understanding that a solution would take time. The tone of the negotiations had improved to the point where the OPEC leaders decided to abandon their threat to stop shipping oil to the West. Slowly, the world moved closer to precrisis normality, and by the end of May the market regained 60 percent of the loss suffered.

In addition to saving their assets, the three couples realized a sizeable gain, and they also learned how fragile life could be. Despite the brief look Jerry got of things to come, the future was still an unknown.

During the hot summer, a partial agreement began to emerge between the Palestinians and Israel. It defined the territory that would make up the new Palestine in exchange for absolute security guarantees to Israel. Israel pledged free access to the holy sites in Jerusalem. There was a proposal to relocate Jewish settlements in the occupied land that would become part of Palestine in exchange for reducing the number of Palestinians who could return to Israel. The balance of the Palestinians who had formally lived in Israel prior to 1948 would have the option to take up residence within Palestine.

Just as soon as this issue was settled, the negotiators would attack the last major obstacle to a lasting peace—East Jerusalem. Unlike the past, world pressure, agreement on the other issues, and the support of the Middle Eastern oil-producing nations enhanced the prospects for a final settlement and peace treaty. Everyone believed that if the Palestinian agreement was completed, peace between Israel and the remaining Middle Eastern countries would soon follow.

The Fourth of July, 2005, was indeed a time for celebration for not only the United States but also the world. For the first time in over two thousand years, a peaceful solution to the most perplexing and profound disagreement among some of the oldest peoples in the world could end. How prophetic: a settlement in the place that the god of all three major religions had chosen as his one special place on all the earth. Jackie and Jerry had a Fourth of July party to celebrate the birth of America as well as the most recent blessings that they and their friends were given by Jerry's brief glimpse into the future.